WORD GIRL ™

THE INCREDIBLE
SHRINKING ALLOWANCE

STEVE YOUNG
COVER ARTIST

SHANNON WATTERS
ASSOCIATE EDITOR

ADAM STAFFARONI
ASSISTANT EDITOR

SPECIAL THANKS TO LYNNE KARPPI, DANIELLE GILLIS, AND GARY HYMOWITZ

kaboom!

Ross Richie - Chief Executive Officer

Matt Gagnon - Editor-in-Chief

Adam Fortier - VP-New Business

Wes Harris - VP-Publishing

Lance Kreiter - VP-Licensing & Merchandising

Bryce Carlson - Managing Editor

Dafna Pleban - Editor

Shannon Watters - Associate Editor

Eric Harburn - Assistant Editor

Adam Staffaroni - Assistant Editor

Chris Rosa - Assistant Editor

Brian Latimer - Lead Graphic Designer

Stephanie Gonzaga - Graphic Designer

Phil Barbaro - Operations

Devin Funches - Marketing & Sales Assistant

THE INCREDIBLE
SHRINKING ALLOWANCE

Chris Karwowski
WRITER

Steve Young
ART AND COLORS

Steve Wands
LETTERS

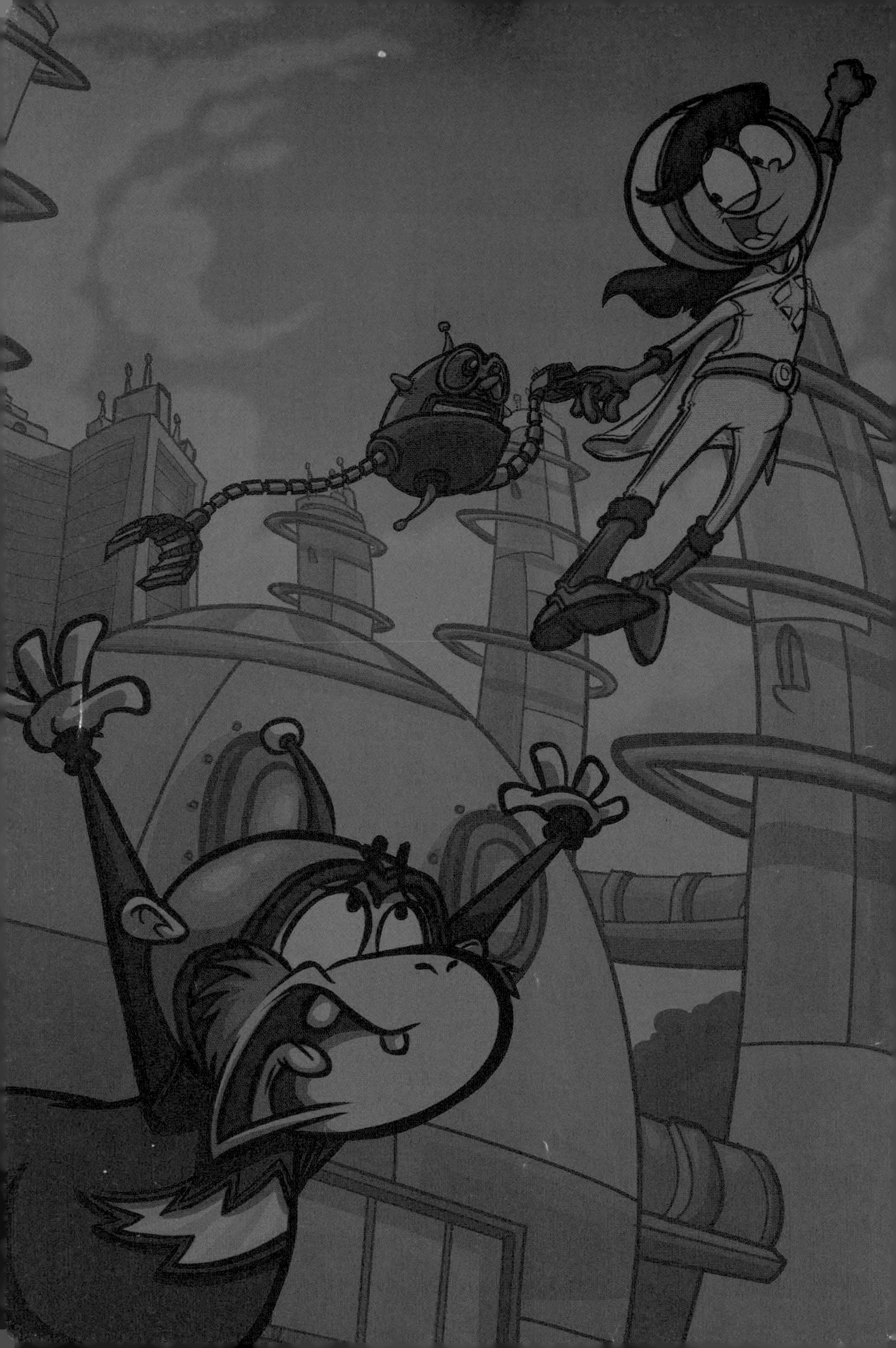

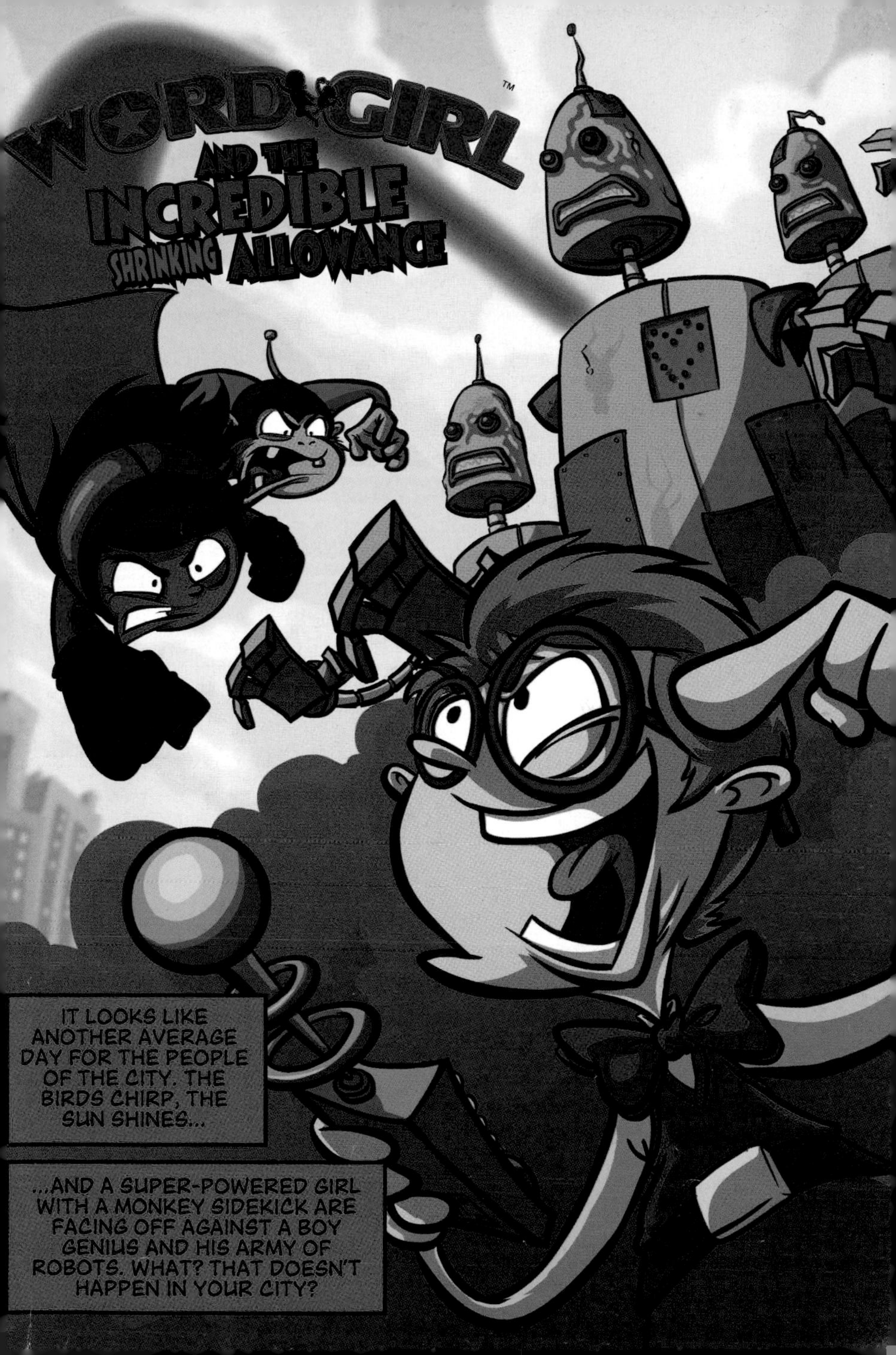
WORDGIRL™
AND THE INCREDIBLE SHRINKING ALLOWANCE
IT LOOKS LIKE ANOTHER AVERAGE DAY FOR THE PEOPLE OF THE CITY. THE BIRDS CHIRP, THE SUN SHINES...
...AND A SUPER-POWERED GIRL WITH A MONKEY SIDEKICK ARE FACING OFF AGAINST A BOY GENIUS AND HIS ARMY OF ROBOTS. WHAT? THAT DOESN'T HAPPEN IN YOUR CITY?

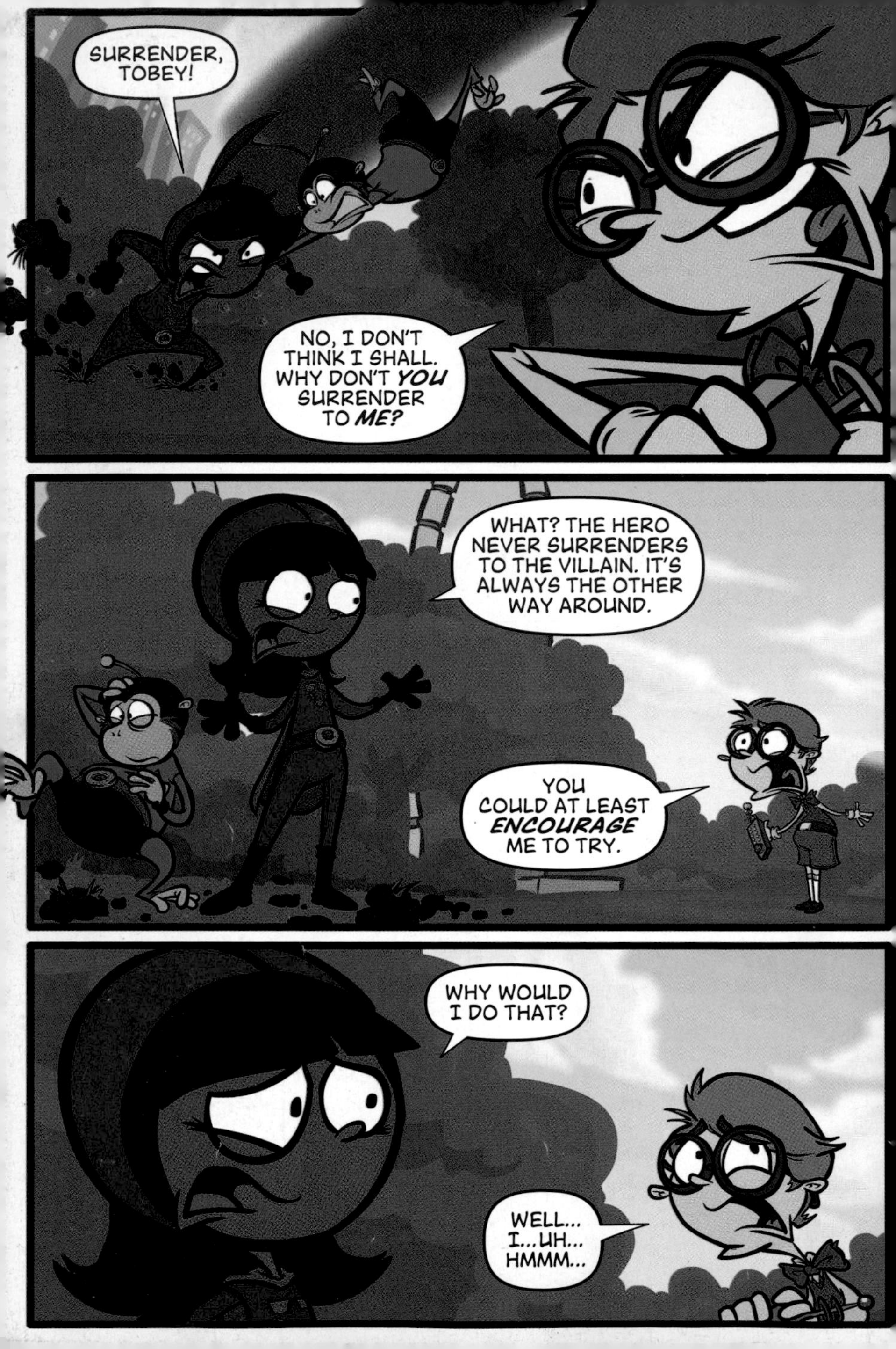
SURRENDER, TOBEY!
NO, I DON'T THINK I SHALL. WHY DON'T *YOU* SURRENDER TO *ME?*
WHAT? THE HERO NEVER SURRENDERS TO THE VILLAIN. IT'S ALWAYS THE OTHER WAY AROUND.
YOU COULD AT LEAST *ENCOURAGE* ME TO TRY.
WHY WOULD I DO THAT?
WELL... I...UH... HMMM...

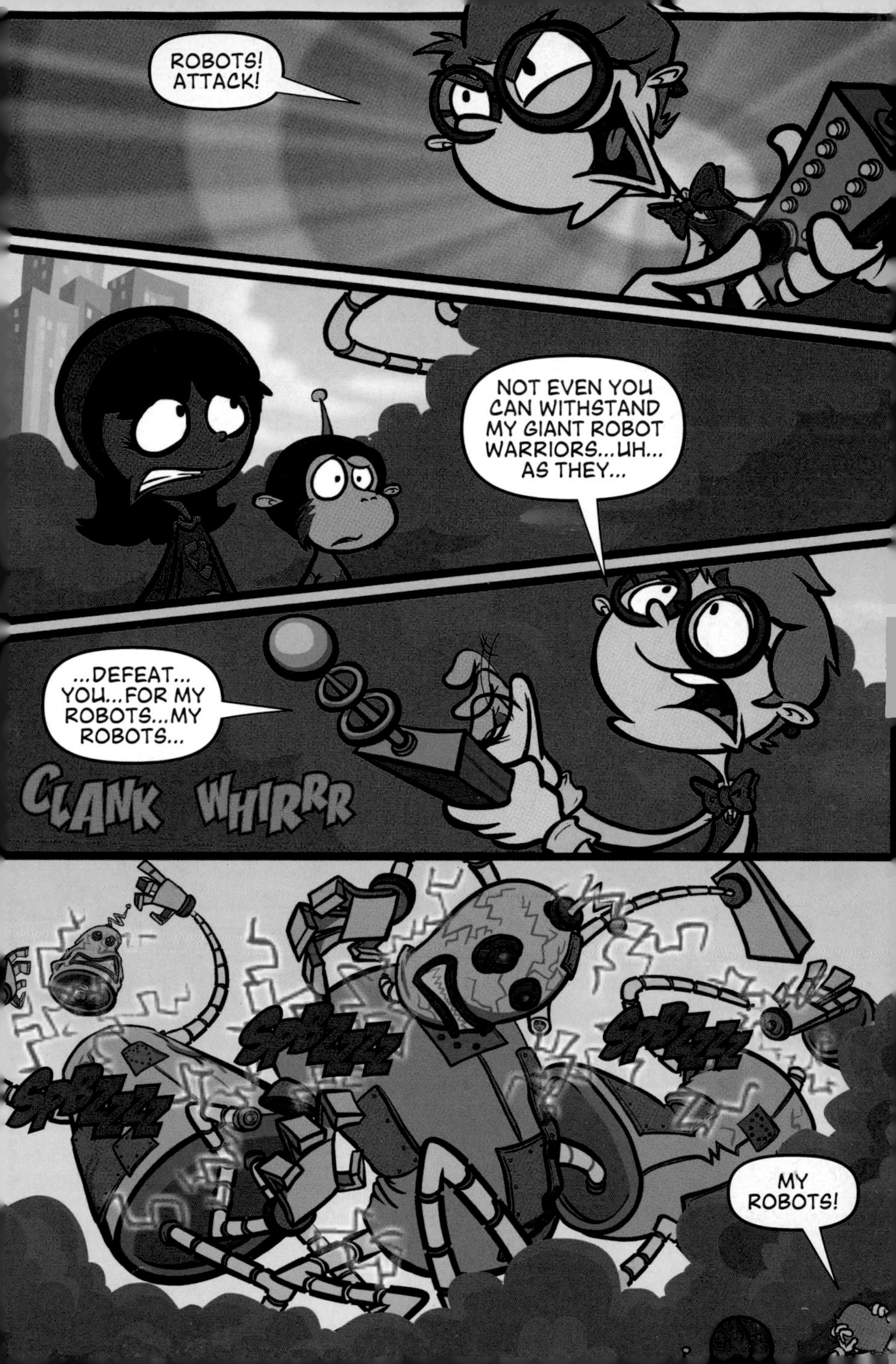
ROBOTS! ATTACK!
NOT EVEN YOU CAN WITHSTAND MY GIANT ROBOT WARRIORS...UH... AS THEY...
...DEFEAT... YOU...FOR MY ROBOTS...MY ROBOTS...
CLANK
WHIRRR
MY ROBOTS!

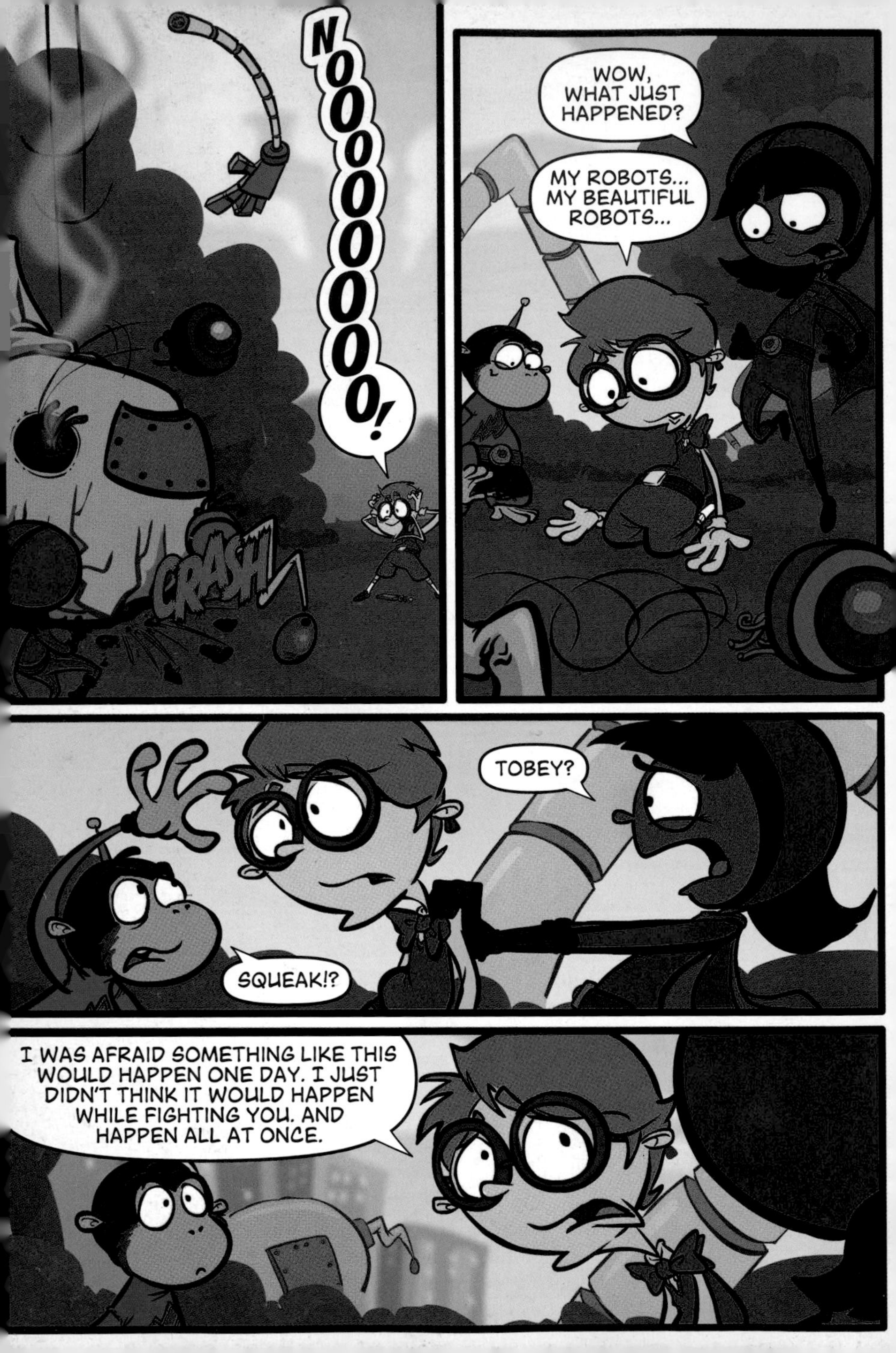
NOOOOOOOOOOO!
CRASH!
WOW, WHAT JUST HAPPENED?
MY ROBOTS... MY BEAUTIFUL ROBOTS...
TOBEY?
SQUEAK!?
I WAS AFRAID SOMETHING LIKE THIS WOULD HAPPEN ONE DAY. I JUST DIDN'T THINK IT WOULD HAPPEN WHILE FIGHTING YOU. AND HAPPEN ALL AT ONCE.

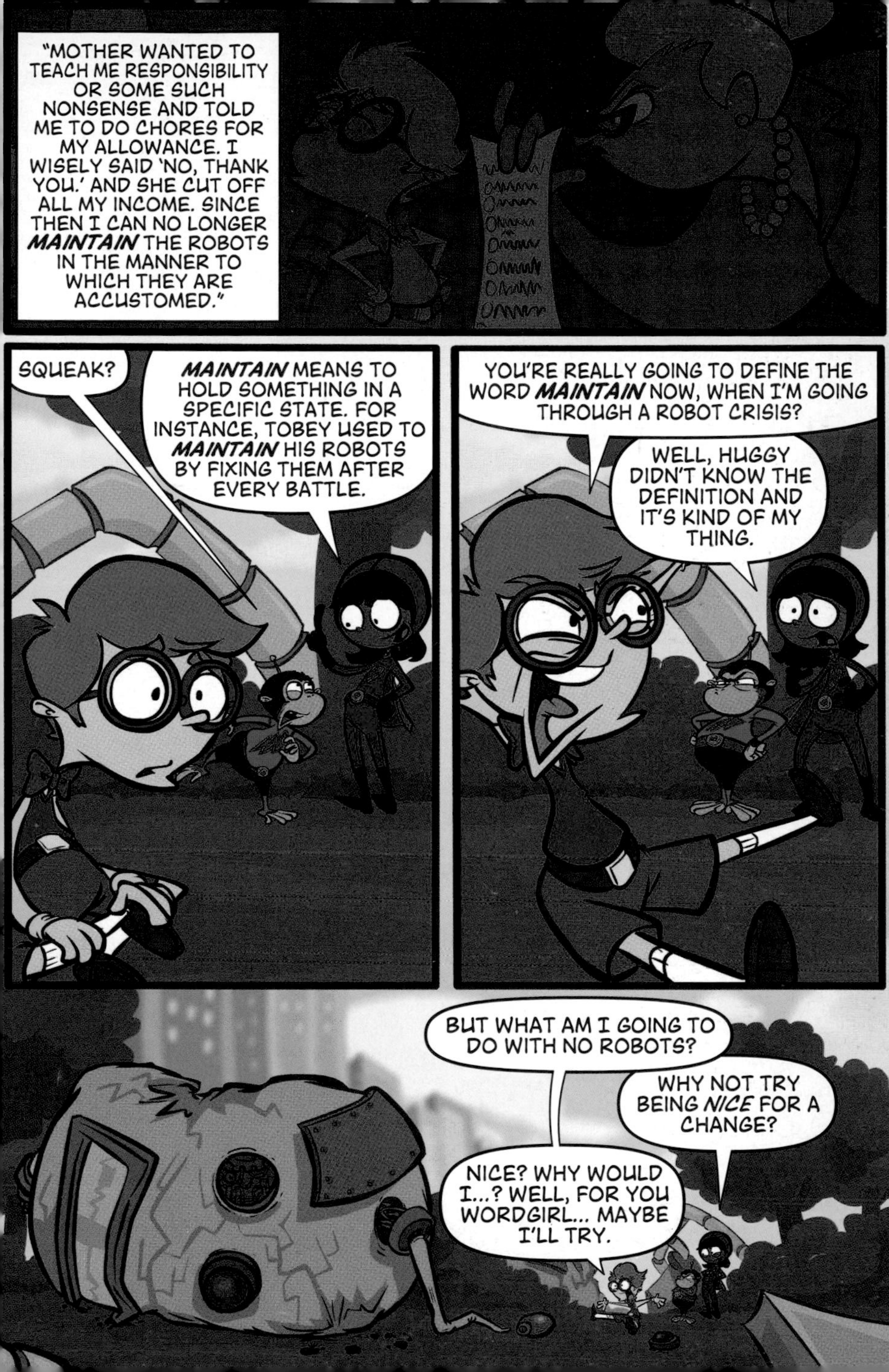
"MOTHER WANTED TO TEACH ME RESPONSIBILITY OR SOME SUCH NONSENSE AND TOLD ME TO DO CHORES FOR MY ALLOWANCE. I WISELY SAID 'NO, THANK YOU.' AND SHE CUT OFF ALL MY INCOME. SINCE THEN I CAN NO LONGER *MAINTAIN* THE ROBOTS IN THE MANNER TO WHICH THEY ARE ACCUSTOMED."
SQUEAK?
MAINTAIN MEANS TO HOLD SOMETHING IN A SPECIFIC STATE. FOR INSTANCE, TOBEY USED TO *MAINTAIN* HIS ROBOTS BY FIXING THEM AFTER EVERY BATTLE.
YOU'RE REALLY GOING TO DEFINE THE WORD *MAINTAIN* NOW, WHEN I'M GOING THROUGH A ROBOT CRISIS?
WELL, HUGGY DIDN'T KNOW THE DEFINITION AND IT'S KIND OF MY THING.
BUT WHAT AM I GOING TO DO WITH NO ROBOTS?
WHY NOT TRY BEING *NICE* FOR A CHANGE?
NICE? WHY WOULD I...? WELL, FOR YOU WORDGIRL... MAYBE I'LL TRY.

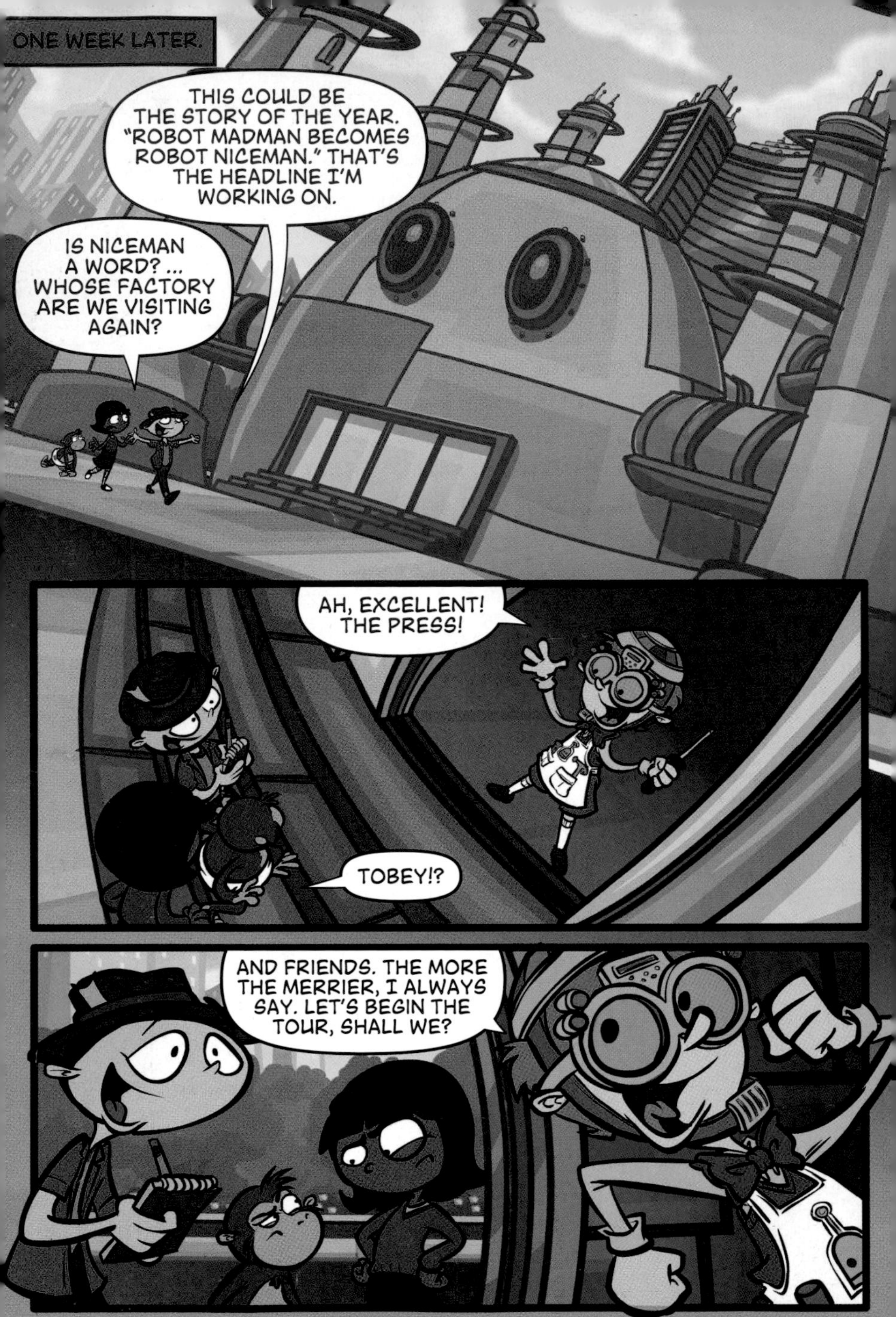
ONE WEEK LATER.
THIS COULD BE THE STORY OF THE YEAR. "ROBOT MADMAN BECOMES ROBOT NICEMAN." THAT'S THE HEADLINE I'M WORKING ON.
IS NICEMAN A WORD? ... WHOSE FACTORY ARE WE VISITING AGAIN?
AH, EXCELLENT! THE PRESS!
TOBEY!?
AND FRIENDS. THE MORE THE MERRIER, I ALWAYS SAY. LET'S BEGIN THE TOUR, SHALL WE?

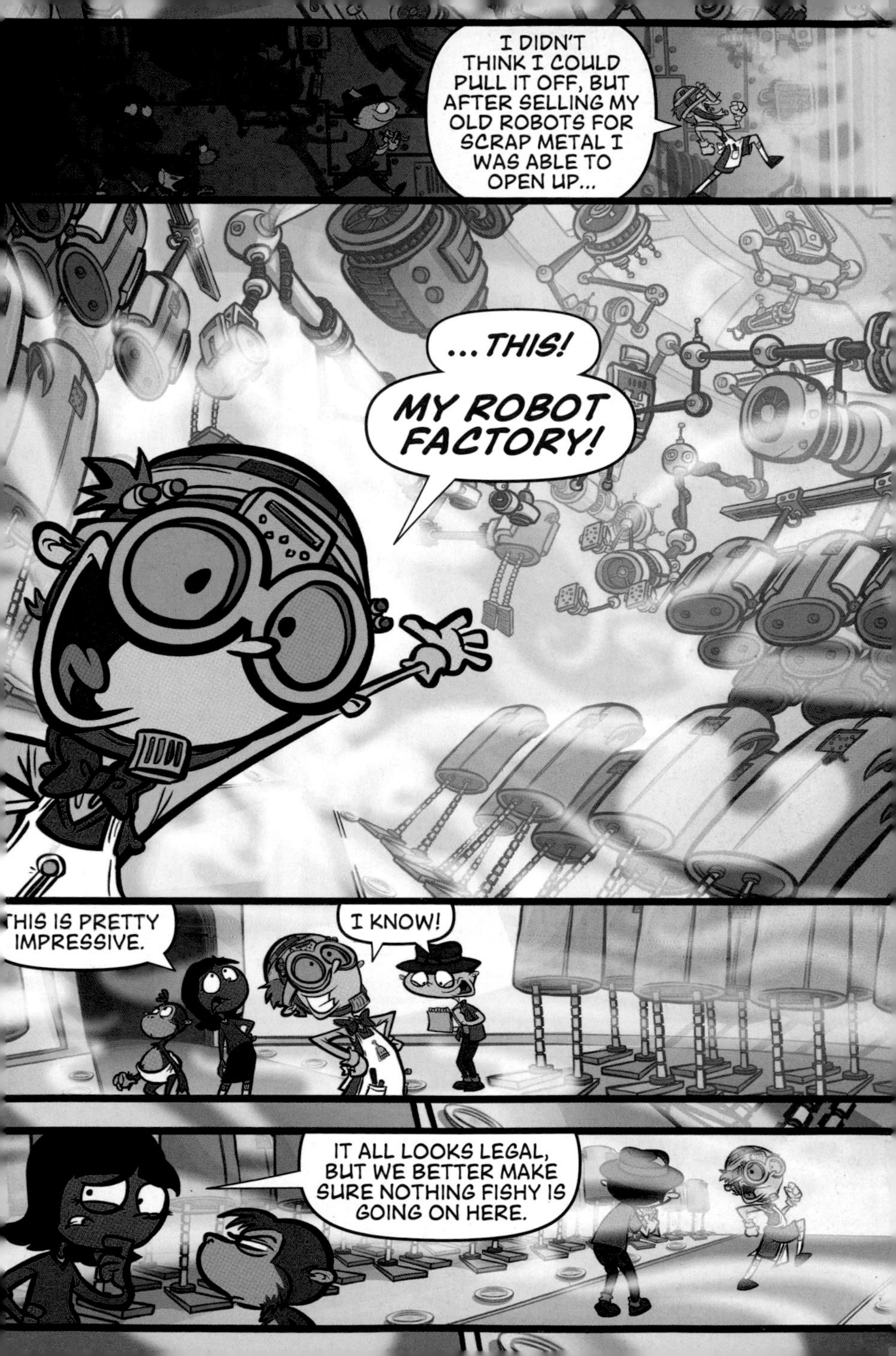
I DIDN'T THINK I COULD PULL IT OFF, BUT AFTER SELLING MY OLD ROBOTS FOR SCRAP METAL I WAS ABLE TO OPEN UP...
...THIS!
MY ROBOT FACTORY!
THIS IS PRETTY IMPRESSIVE.
I KNOW!
IT ALL LOOKS LEGAL, BUT WE BETTER MAKE SURE NOTHING FISHY IS GOING ON HERE.

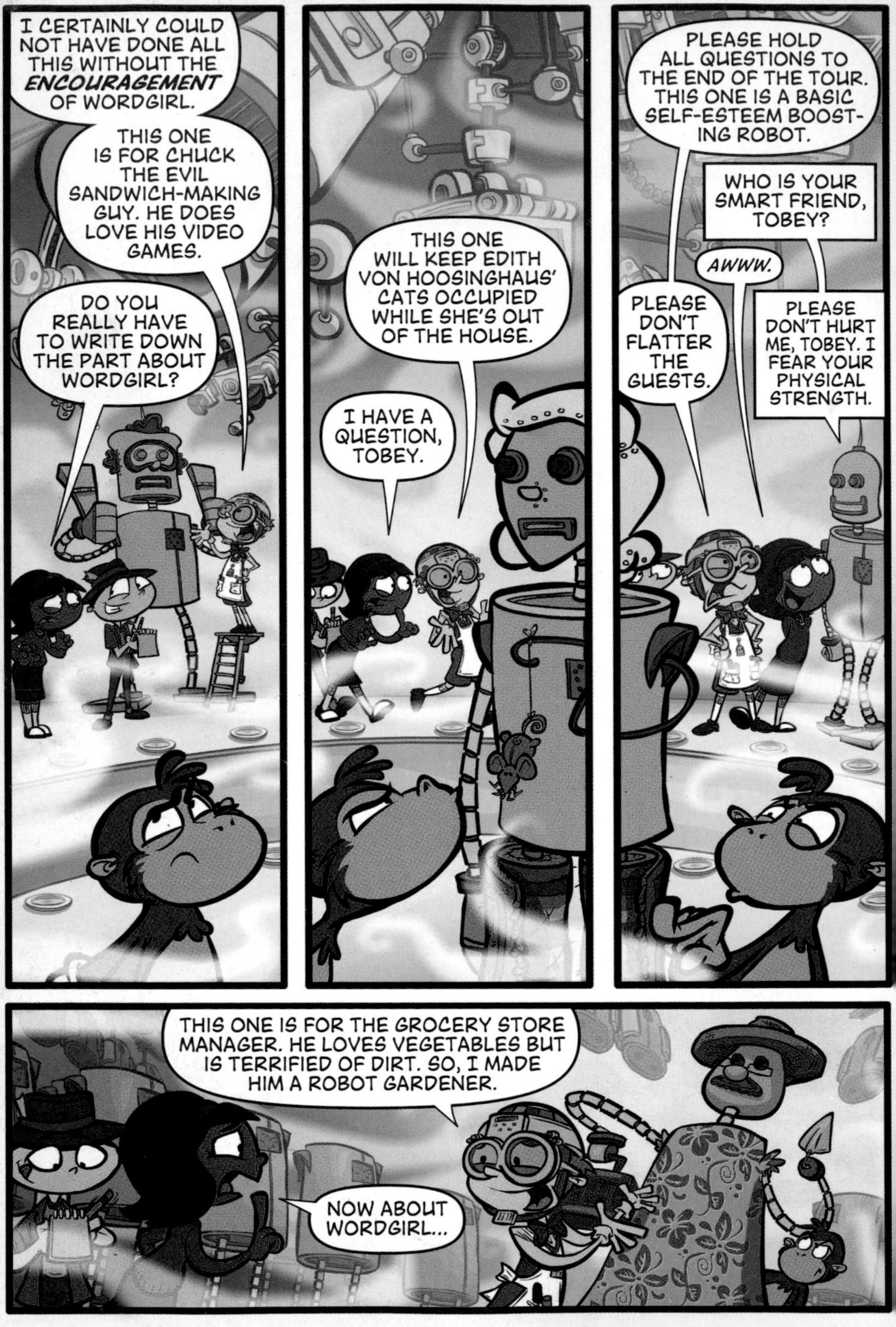
I CERTAINLY COULD NOT HAVE DONE ALL THIS WITHOUT THE *ENCOURAGEMENT* OF WORDGIRL.
THIS ONE IS FOR CHUCK THE EVIL SANDWICH-MAKING GUY. HE DOES LOVE HIS VIDEO GAMES.
DO YOU REALLY HAVE TO WRITE DOWN THE PART ABOUT WORDGIRL?
THIS ONE WILL KEEP EDITH VON HOOSINGHAUS' CATS OCCUPIED WHILE SHE'S OUT OF THE HOUSE.
I HAVE A QUESTION, TOBEY.
PLEASE HOLD ALL QUESTIONS TO THE END OF THE TOUR. THIS ONE IS A BASIC SELF-ESTEEM BOOSTING ROBOT.
WHO IS YOUR SMART FRIEND, TOBEY?
AWWW.
PLEASE DON'T FLATTER THE GUESTS.
PLEASE DON'T HURT ME, TOBEY. I FEAR YOUR PHYSICAL STRENGTH.
THIS ONE IS FOR THE GROCERY STORE MANAGER. HE LOVES VEGETABLES BUT IS TERRIFIED OF DIRT. SO, I MADE HIM A ROBOT GARDENER.
NOW ABOUT WORDGIRL...

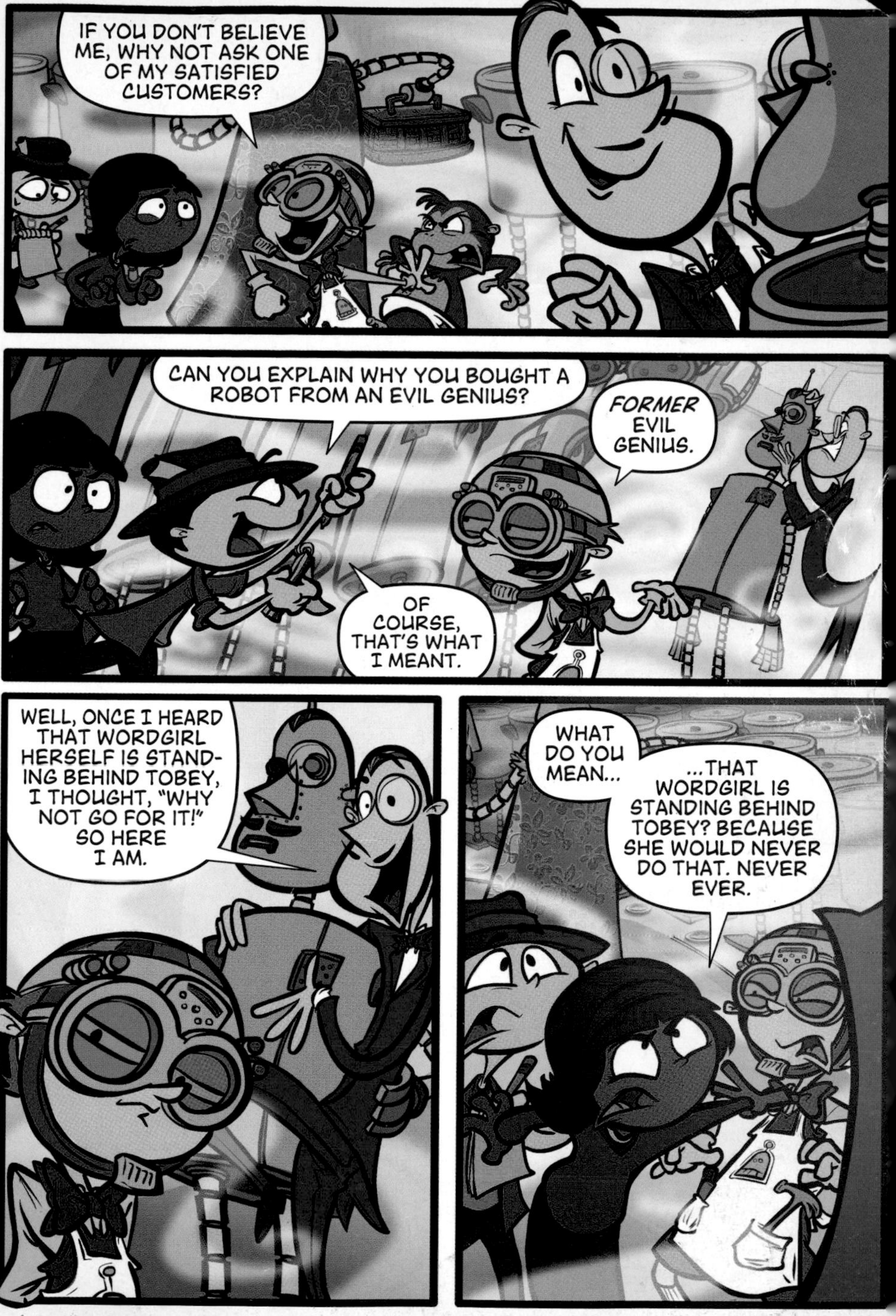
IF YOU DON'T BELIEVE ME, WHY NOT ASK ONE OF MY SATISFIED CUSTOMERS?
CAN YOU EXPLAIN WHY YOU BOUGHT A ROBOT FROM AN EVIL GENIUS?
FORMER EVIL GENIUS.
OF COURSE, THAT'S WHAT I MEANT.
WELL, ONCE I HEARD THAT WORDGIRL HERSELF IS STANDING BEHIND TOBEY, I THOUGHT, "WHY NOT GO FOR IT!" SO HERE I AM.
WHAT DO YOU MEAN...
...THAT WORDGIRL IS STANDING BEHIND TOBEY? BECAUSE SHE WOULD NEVER DO THAT. NEVER EVER.

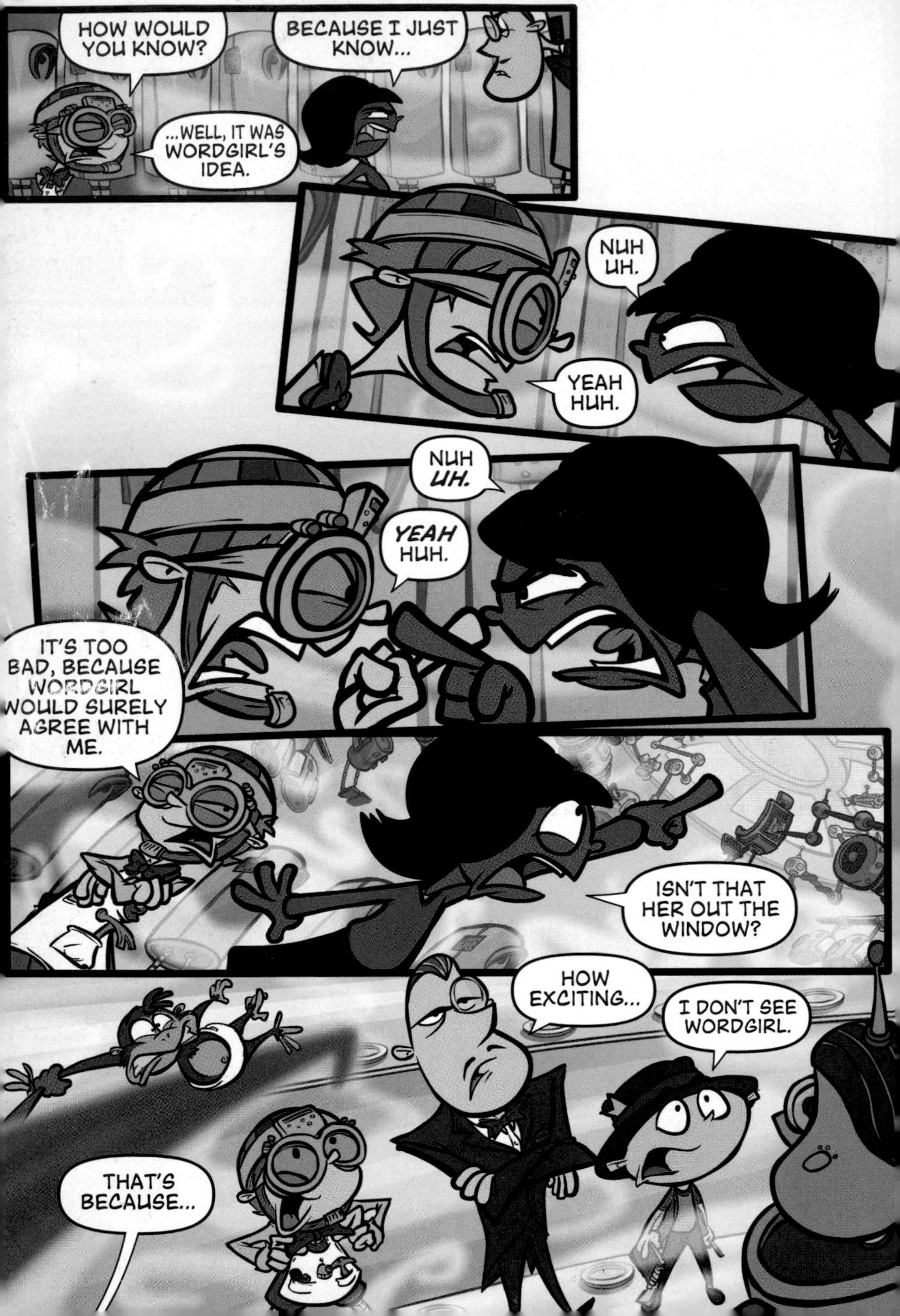
HOW WOULD YOU KNOW?
BECAUSE I JUST KNOW...
...WELL, IT WAS WORDGIRL'S IDEA.
NUH UH.
YEAH HUH.
NUH *UH.*
YEAH HUH.
IT'S TOO BAD, BECAUSE WORDGIRL WOULD SURELY AGREE WITH ME.
ISN'T THAT HER OUT THE WINDOW?
HOW EXCITING...
I DON'T SEE WORDGIRL.
THAT'S BECAUSE...

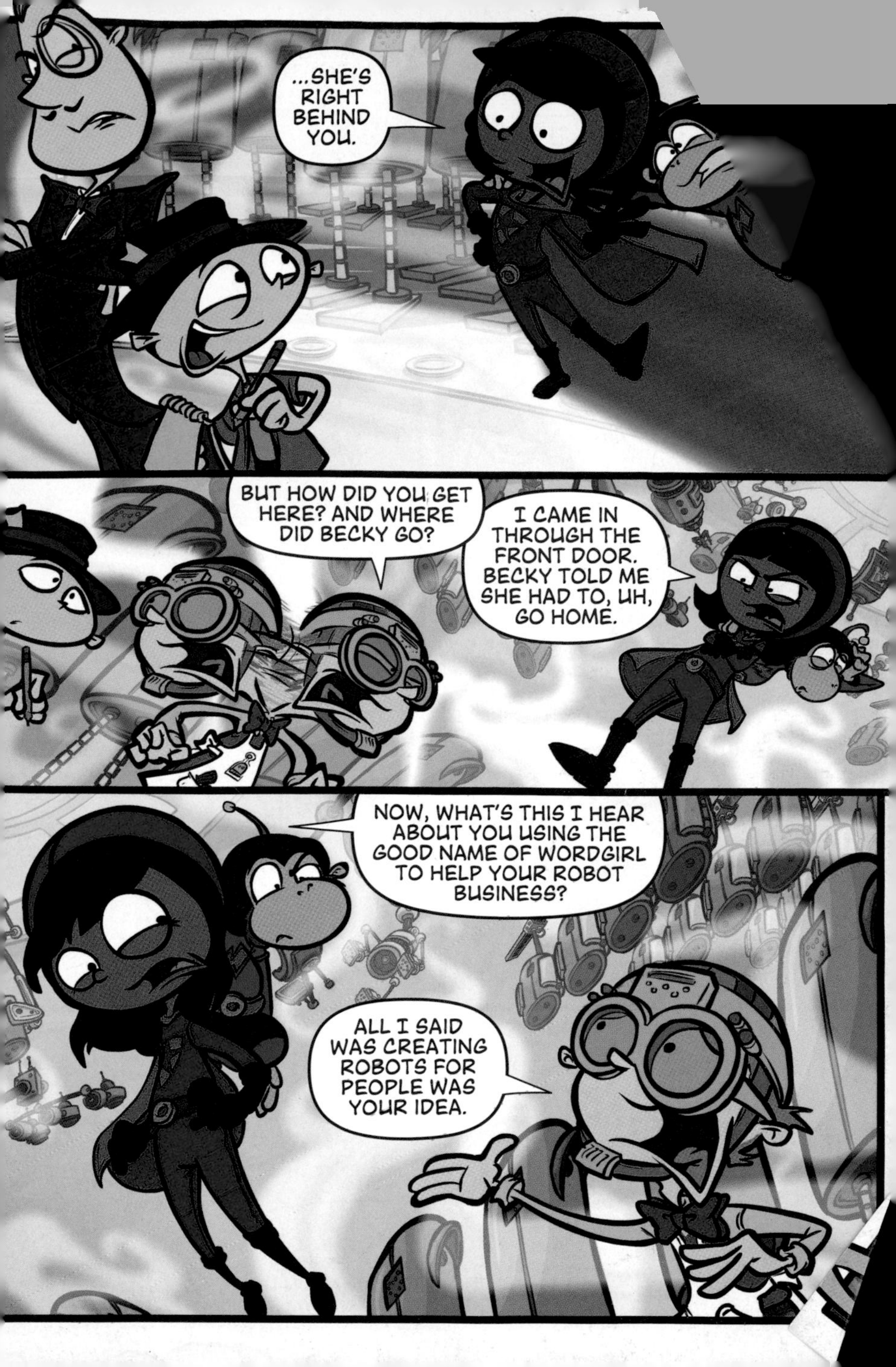
...SHE'S RIGHT BEHIND YOU.
BUT HOW DID YOU GET HERE? AND WHERE DID BECKY GO?
I CAME IN THROUGH THE FRONT DOOR. BECKY TOLD ME SHE HAD TO, UH, GO HOME.
NOW, WHAT'S THIS I HEAR ABOUT YOU USING THE GOOD NAME OF WORDGIRL TO HELP YOUR ROBOT BUSINESS?
ALL I SAID WAS CREATING ROBOTS FOR PEOPLE WAS YOUR IDEA.

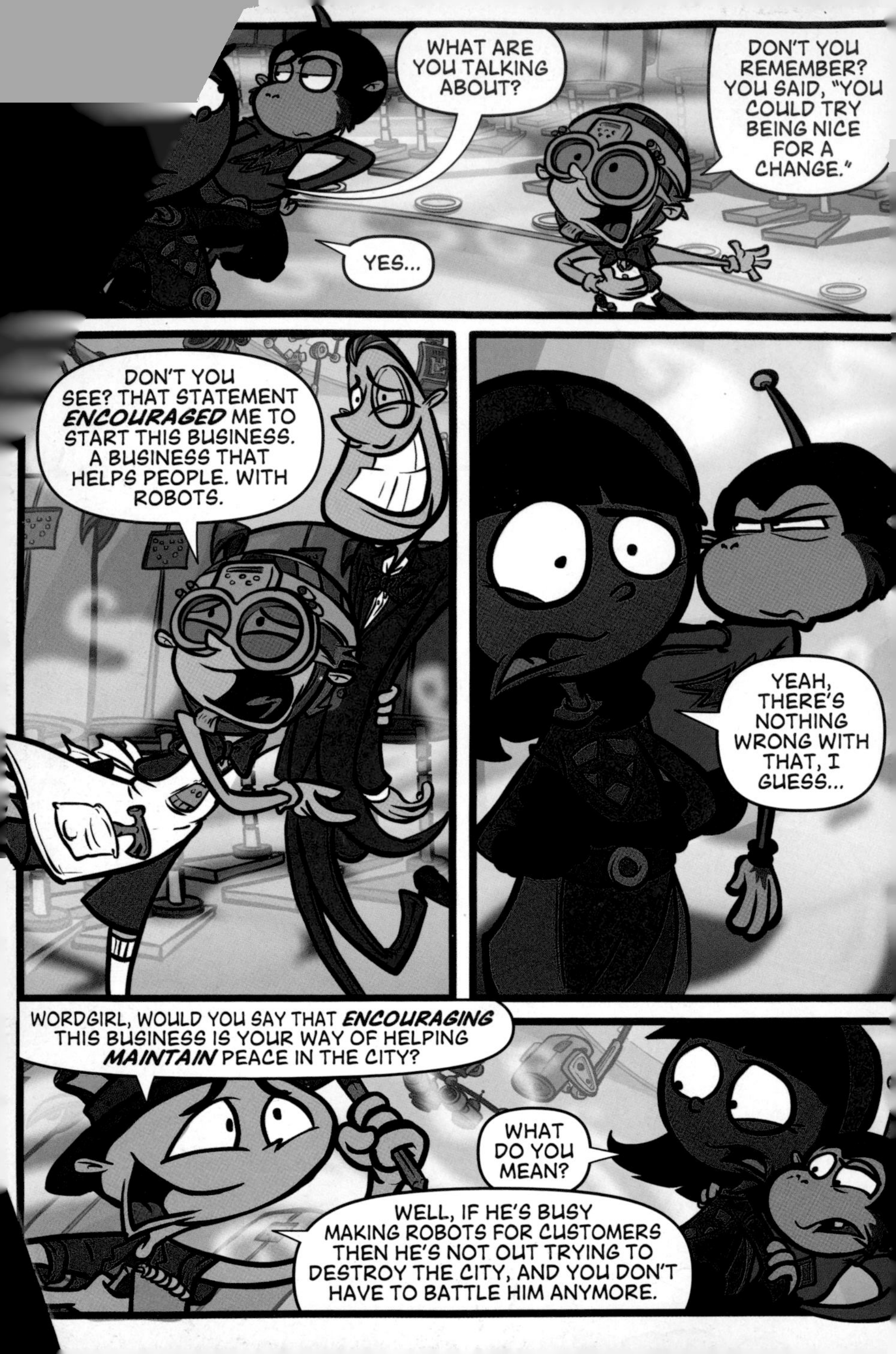
WHAT ARE YOU TALKING ABOUT?
DON'T YOU REMEMBER? YOU SAID, "YOU COULD TRY BEING NICE FOR A CHANGE."
YES...
DON'T YOU SEE? THAT STATEMENT ENCOURAGED ME TO START THIS BUSINESS. A BUSINESS THAT HELPS PEOPLE. WITH ROBOTS.
YEAH, THERE'S NOTHING WRONG WITH THAT, I GUESS...
WORDGIRL, WOULD YOU SAY THAT ENCOURAGING THIS BUSINESS IS YOUR WAY OF HELPING MAINTAIN PEACE IN THE CITY?
WHAT DO YOU MEAN?
WELL, IF HE'S BUSY MAKING ROBOTS FOR CUSTOMERS THEN HE'S NOT OUT TRYING TO DESTROY THE CITY, AND YOU DON'T HAVE TO BATTLE HIM ANYMORE.

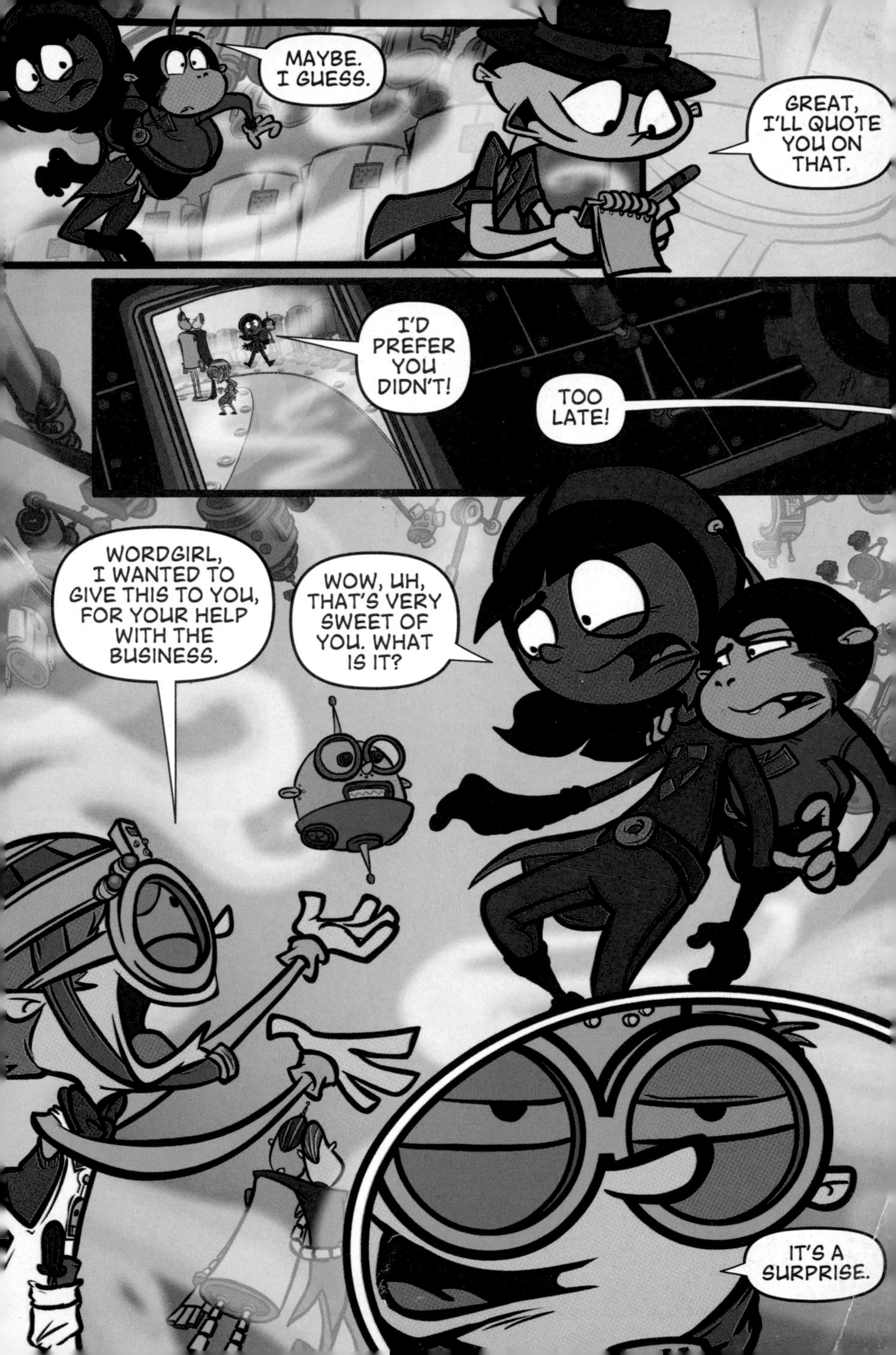
MAYBE. I GUESS.
GREAT, I'LL QUOTE YOU ON THAT.
I'D PREFER YOU DIDN'T!
TOO LATE!
WORDGIRL, I WANTED TO GIVE THIS TO YOU, FOR YOUR HELP WITH THE BUSINESS.
WOW, UH, THAT'S VERY SWEET OF YOU. WHAT IS IT?
IT'S A SURPRISE.

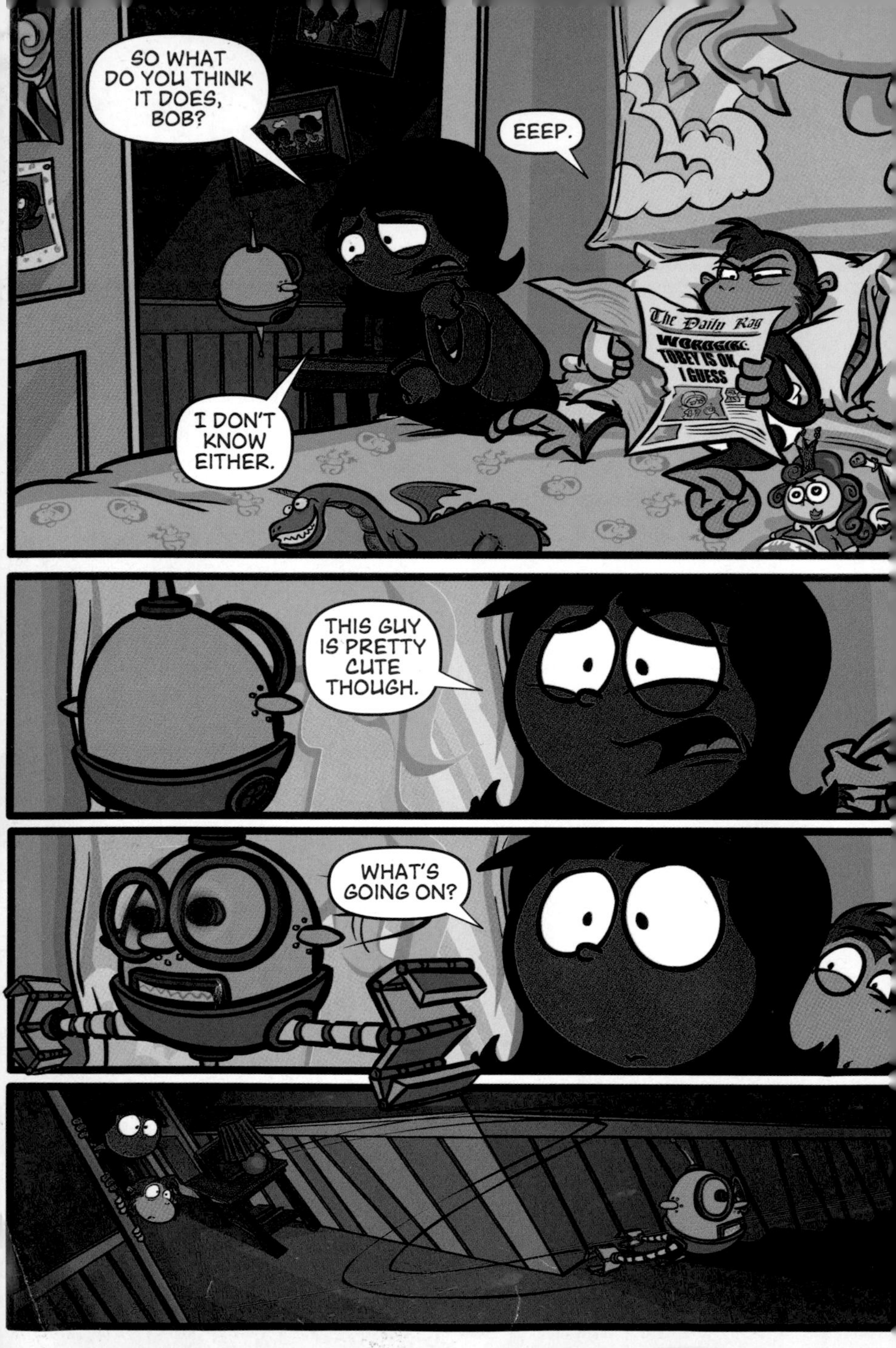
SO WHAT DO YOU THINK IT DOES, BOB?
EEEP.
The Daily Rag
WORDGIRL: TOBEY IS OK, I GUESS
I DON'T KNOW EITHER.
THIS GUY IS PRETTY CUTE THOUGH.
WHAT'S GOING ON?

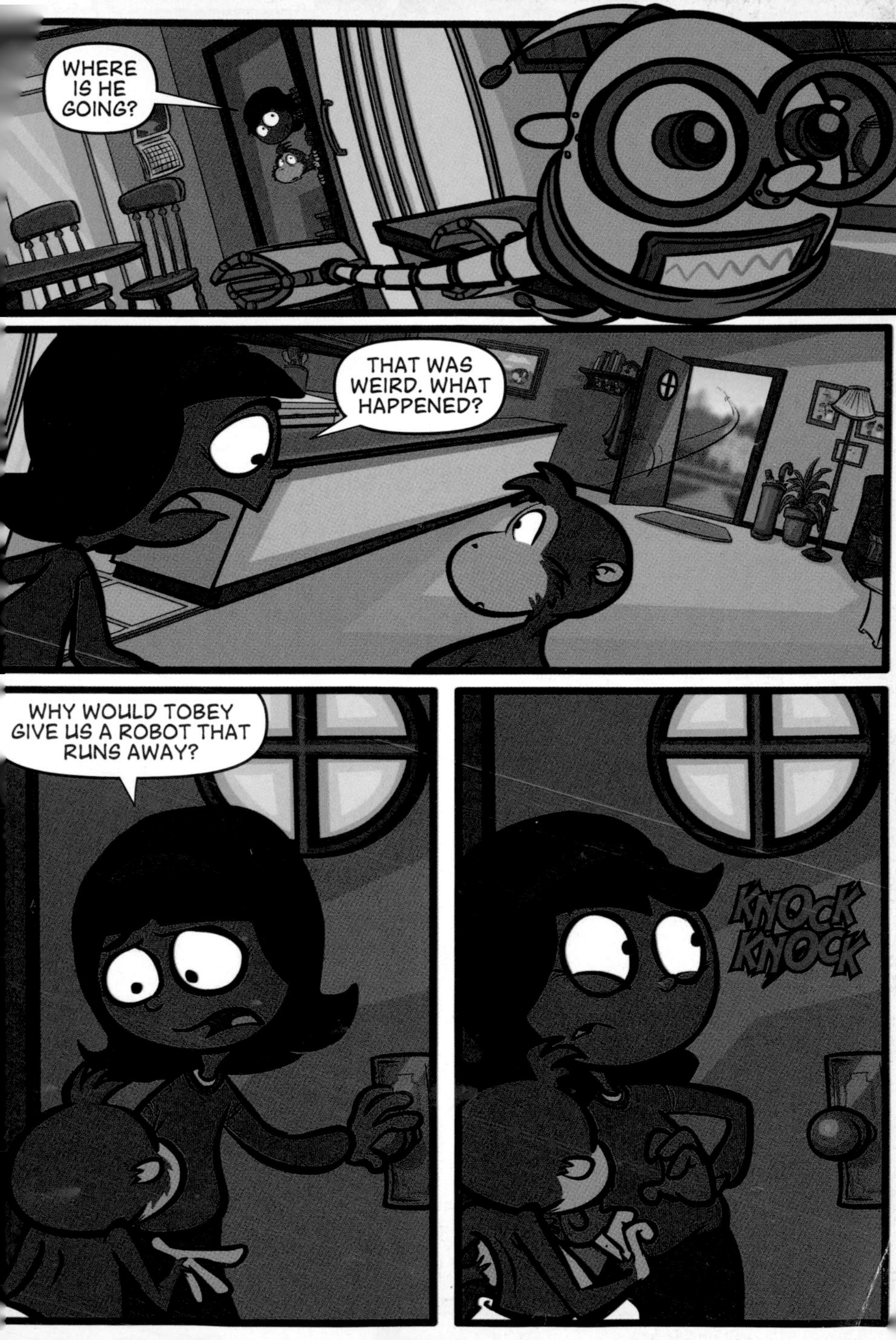
WHERE IS HE GOING?
THAT WAS WEIRD. WHAT HAPPENED?
WHY WOULD TOBEY GIVE US A ROBOT THAT RUNS AWAY?
KNOCK KNOCK

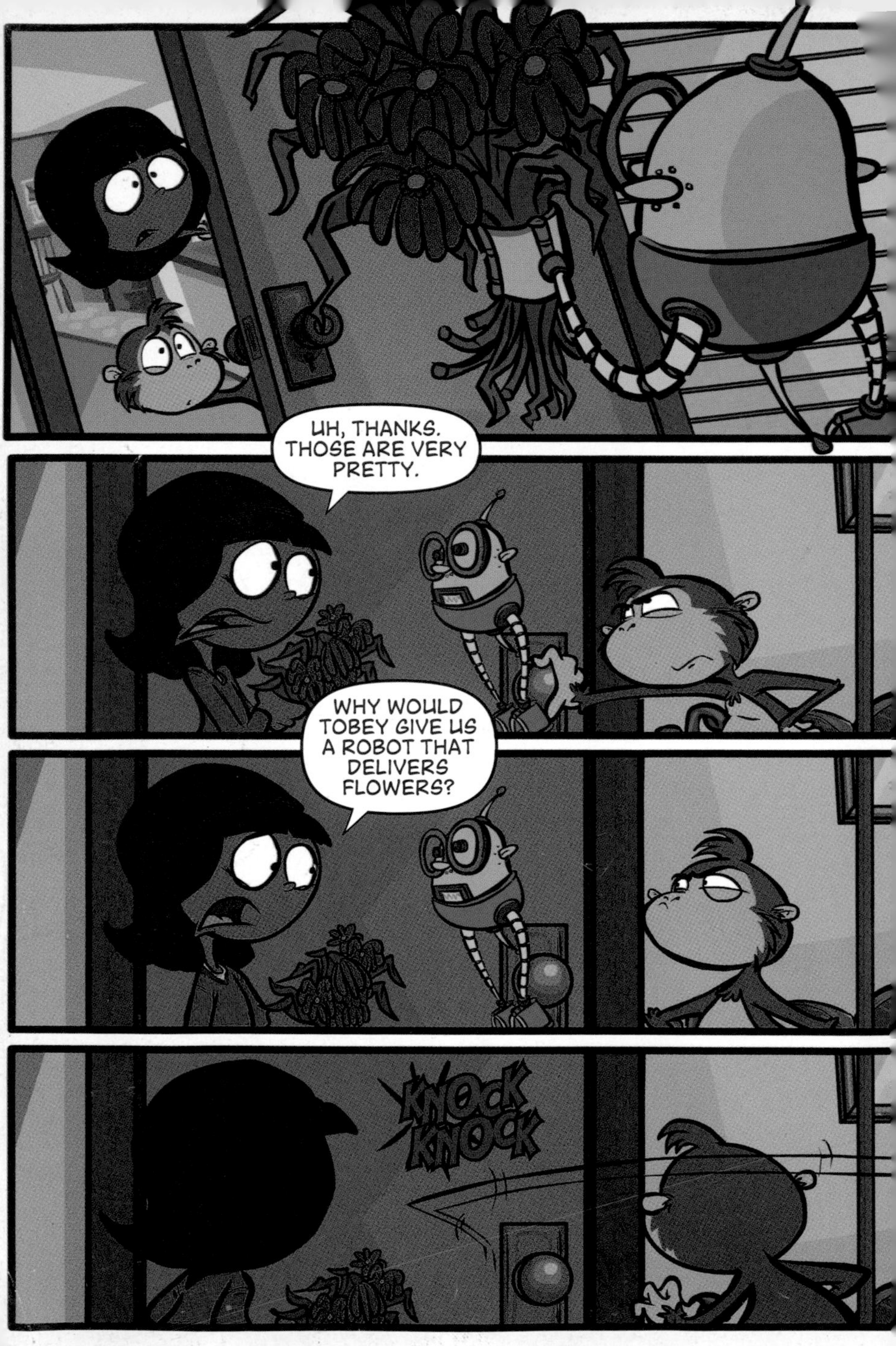
UH, THANKS. THOSE ARE VERY PRETTY.
WHY WOULD TOBEY GIVE US A ROBOT THAT DELIVERS FLOWERS?
KNOCK KNOCK

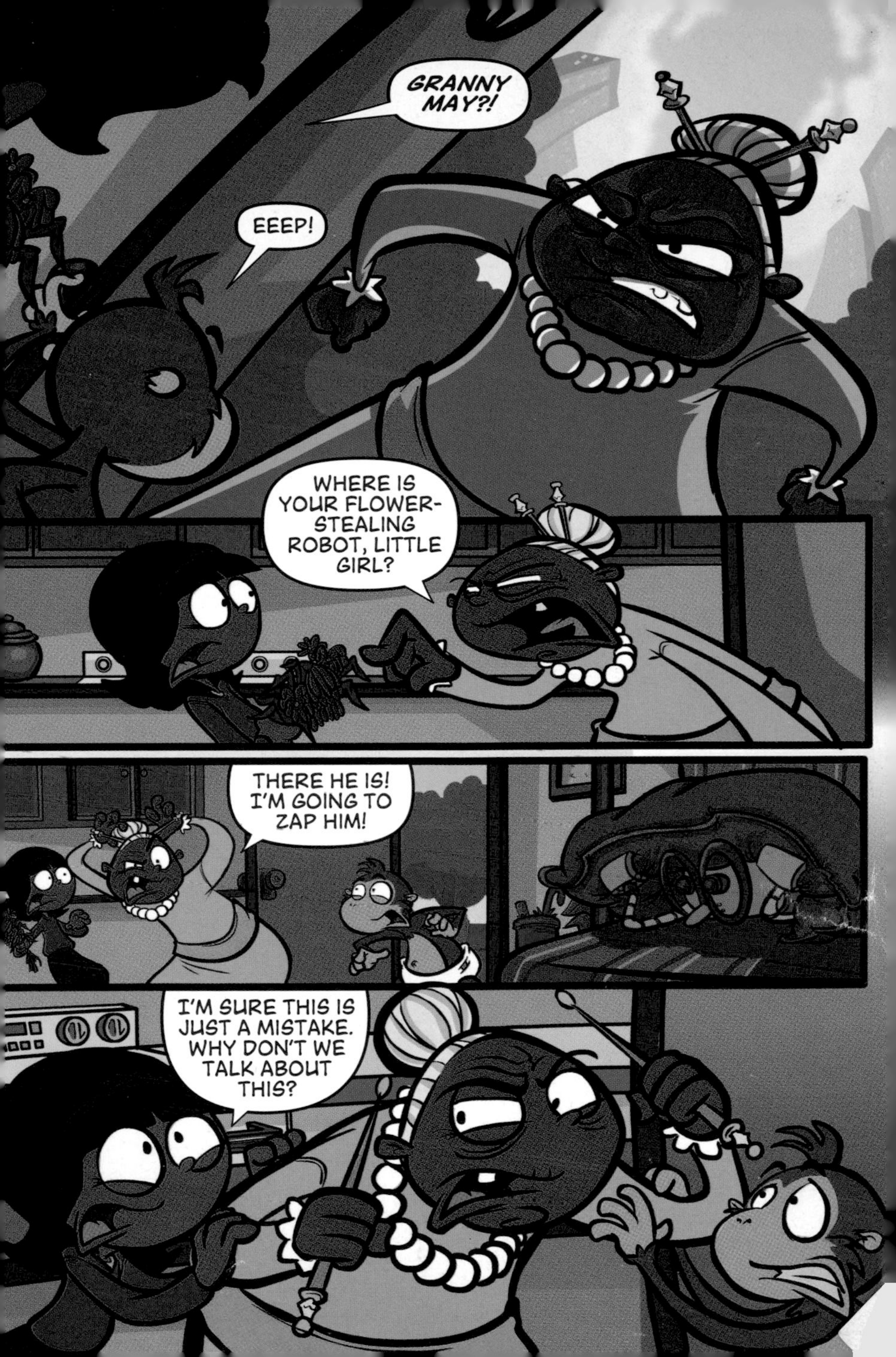
GRANNY MAY?!
EEEP!
WHERE IS YOUR FLOWER-STEALING ROBOT, LITTLE GIRL?
THERE HE IS! I'M GOING TO ZAP HIM!
I'M SURE THIS IS JUST A MISTAKE. WHY DON'T WE TALK ABOUT THIS?

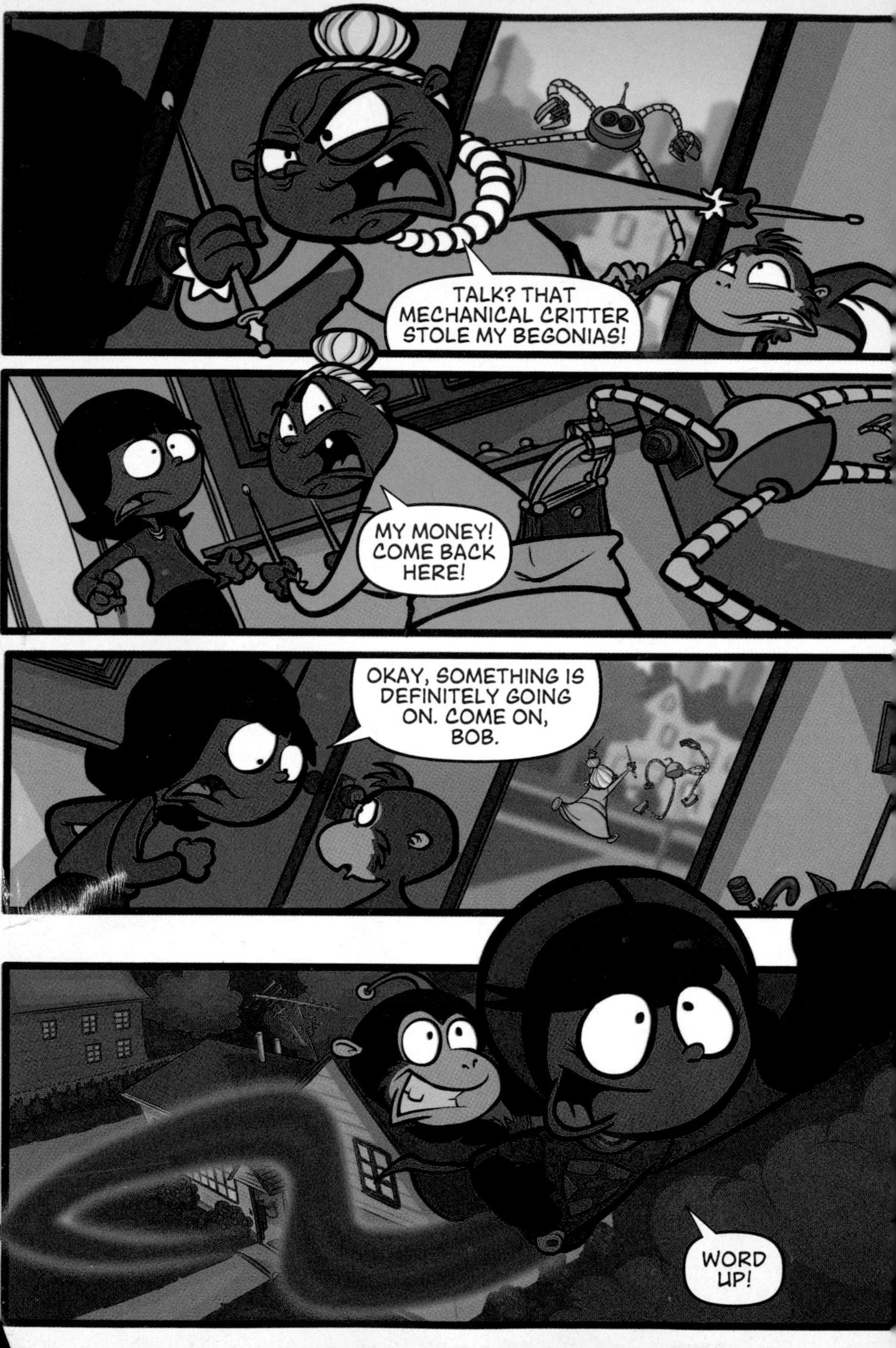
TALK? THAT MECHANICAL CRITTER STOLE MY BEGONIAS!
MY MONEY! COME BACK HERE!
OKAY, SOMETHING IS DEFINITELY GOING ON. COME ON, BOB.
WORD UP!

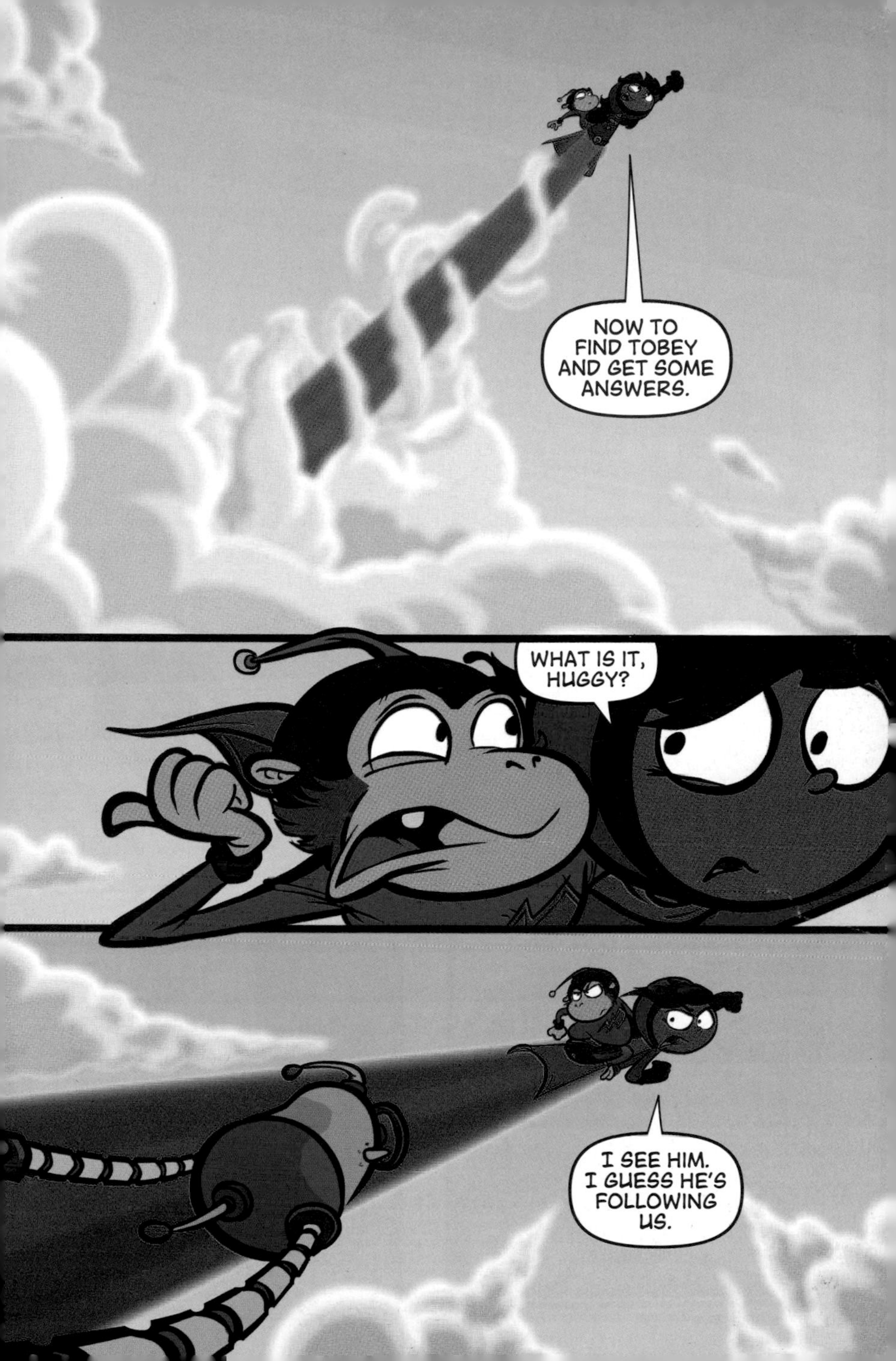
NOW TO FIND TOBEY AND GET SOME ANSWERS.
WHAT IS IT, HUGGY?
I SEE HIM. I GUESS HE'S FOLLOWING US.

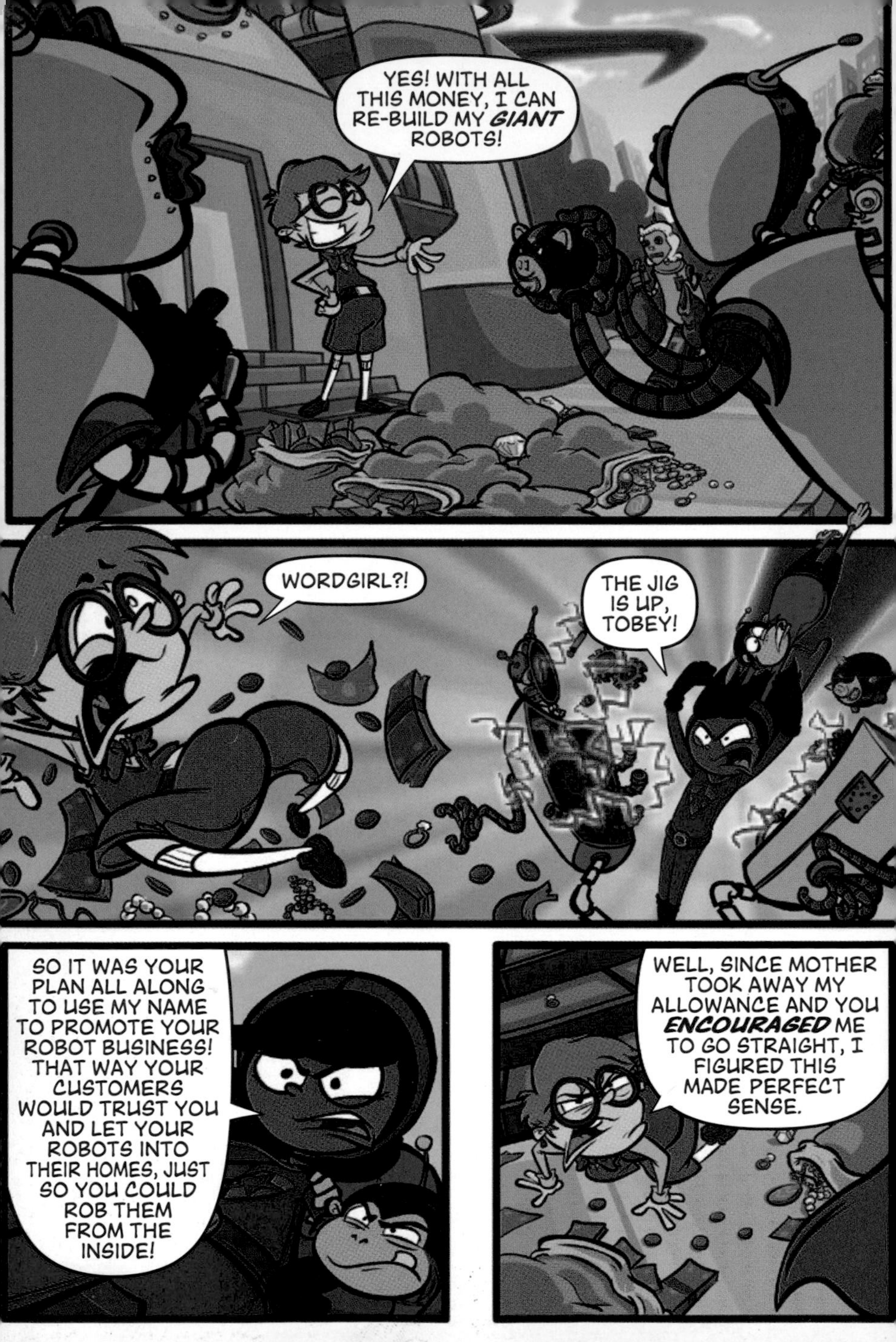
YES! WITH ALL THIS MONEY, I CAN RE-BUILD MY *GIANT* ROBOTS!
WORDGIRL?!
THE JIG IS UP, TOBEY!
SO IT WAS YOUR PLAN ALL ALONG TO USE MY NAME TO PROMOTE YOUR ROBOT BUSINESS! THAT WAY YOUR CUSTOMERS WOULD TRUST YOU AND LET YOUR ROBOTS INTO THEIR HOMES, JUST SO YOU COULD ROB THEM FROM THE INSIDE!
WELL, SINCE MOTHER TOOK AWAY MY ALLOWANCE AND YOU *ENCOURAGED* ME TO GO STRAIGHT, I FIGURED THIS MADE PERFECT SENSE.

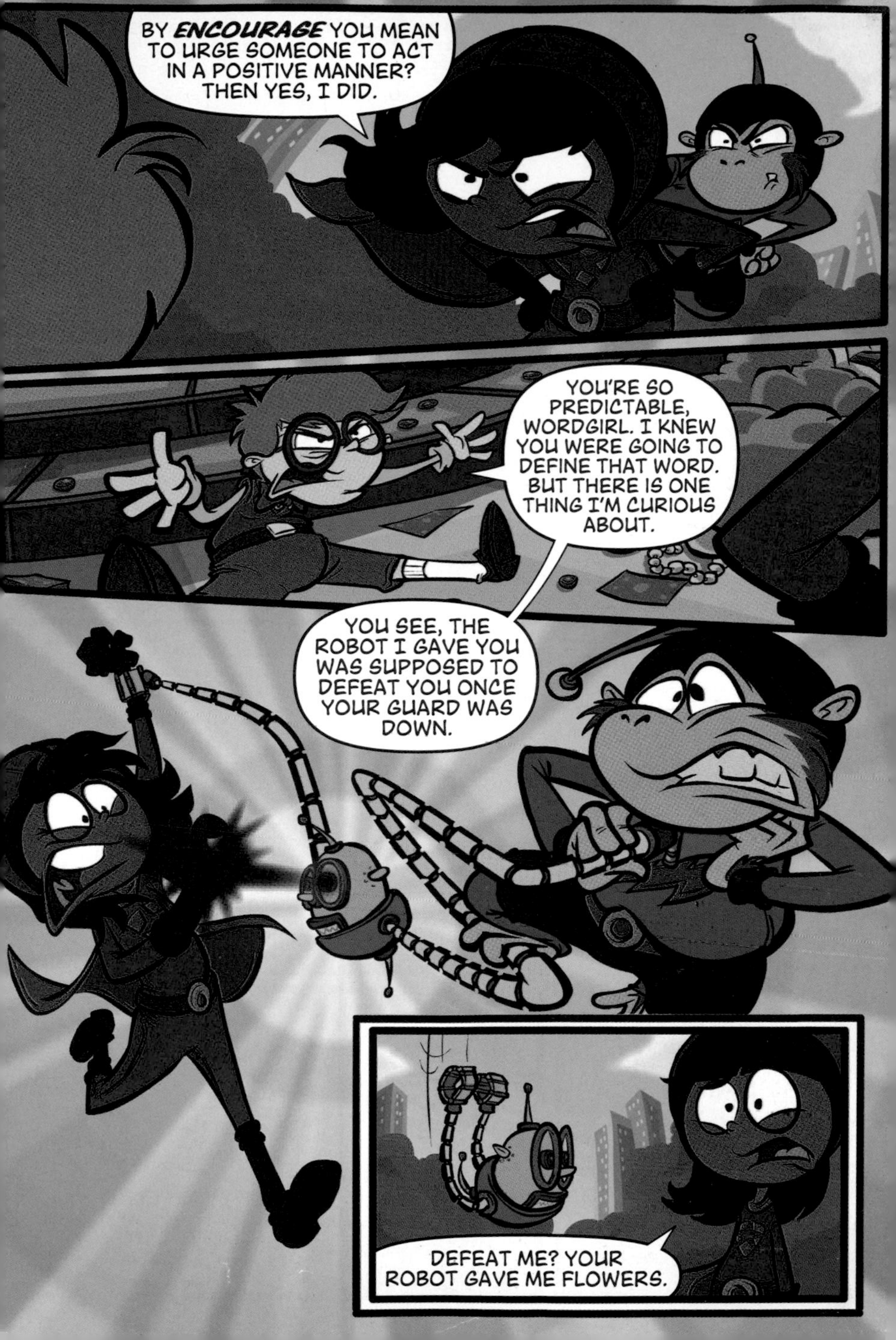
BY ENCOURAGE YOU MEAN TO URGE SOMEONE TO ACT IN A POSITIVE MANNER? THEN YES, I DID.
YOU'RE SO PREDICTABLE, WORDGIRL. I KNEW YOU WERE GOING TO DEFINE THAT WORD. BUT THERE IS ONE THING I'M CURIOUS ABOUT.
YOU SEE, THE ROBOT I GAVE YOU WAS SUPPOSED TO DEFEAT YOU ONCE YOUR GUARD WAS DOWN.
DEFEAT ME? YOUR ROBOT GAVE ME FLOWERS.

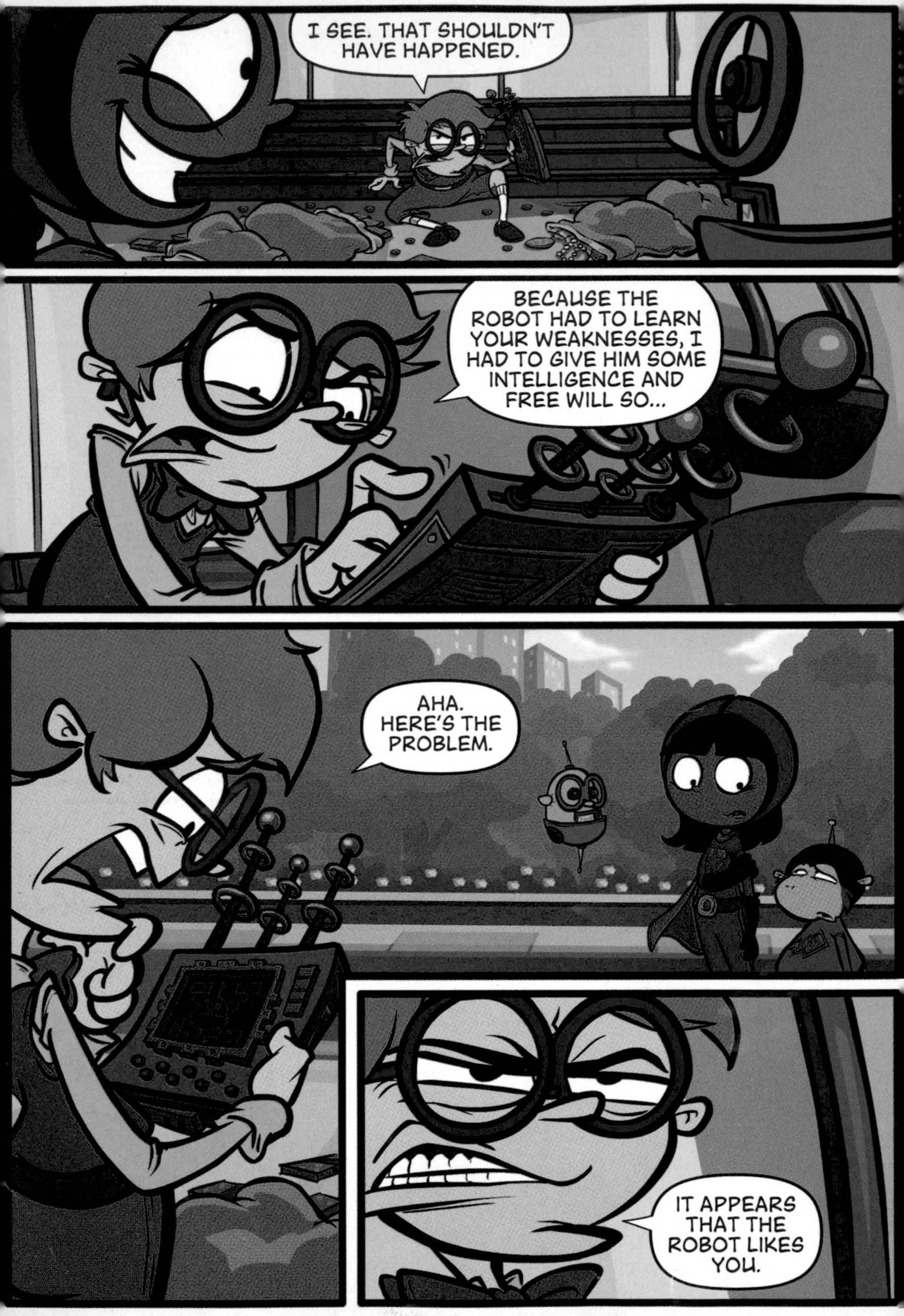
I SEE. THAT SHOULDN'T HAVE HAPPENED.
BECAUSE THE ROBOT HAD TO LEARN YOUR WEAKNESSES, I HAD TO GIVE HIM SOME INTELLIGENCE AND FREE WILL SO...
AHA. HERE'S THE PROBLEM.
IT APPEARS THAT THE ROBOT LIKES YOU.

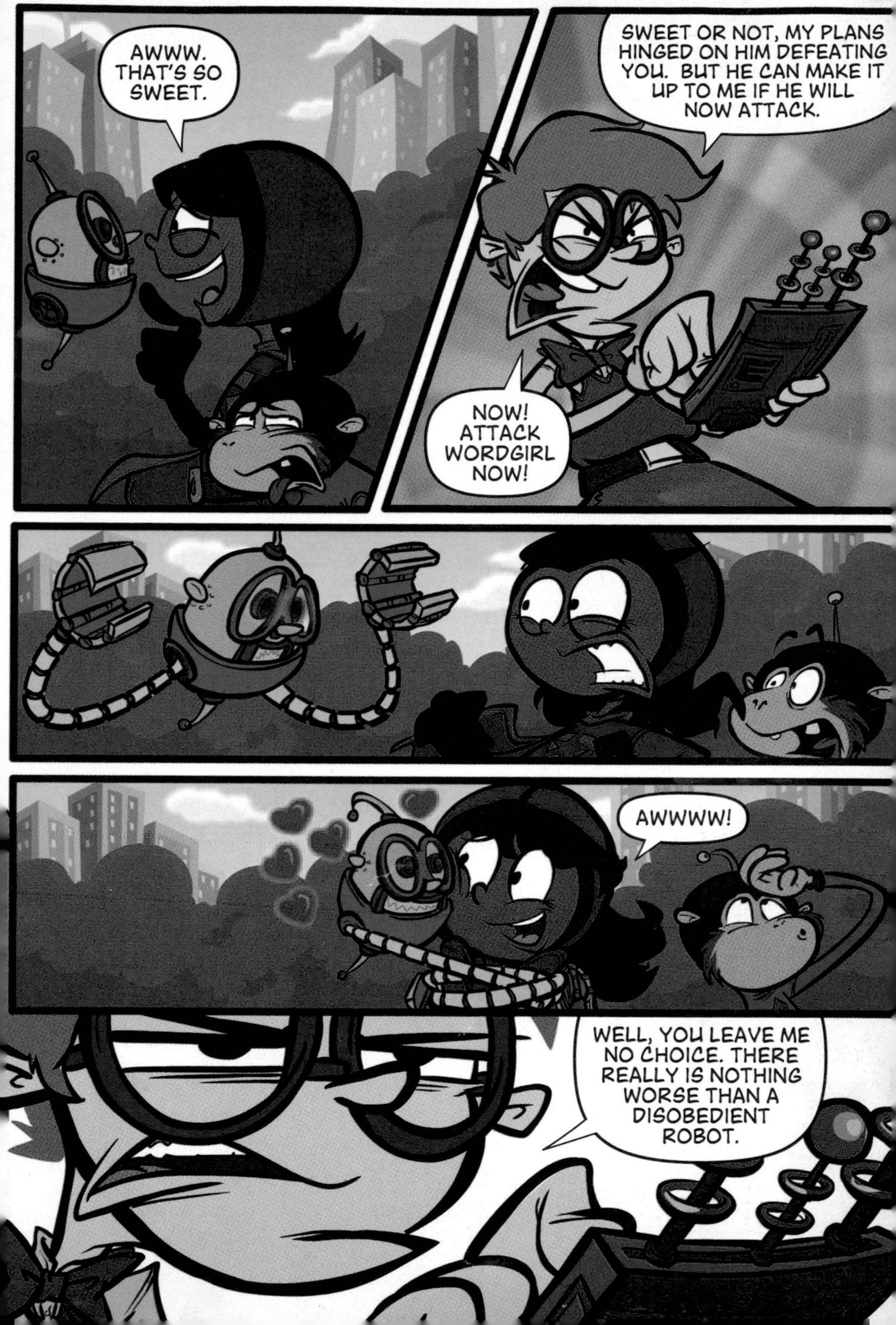
AWWW. THAT'S SO SWEET.
SWEET OR NOT, MY PLANS HINGED ON HIM DEFEATING YOU. BUT HE CAN MAKE IT UP TO ME IF HE WILL NOW ATTACK.
NOW! ATTACK WORDGIRL NOW!
AWWWW!
WELL, YOU LEAVE ME NO CHOICE. THERE REALLY IS NOTHING WORSE THAN A DISOBEDIENT ROBOT.

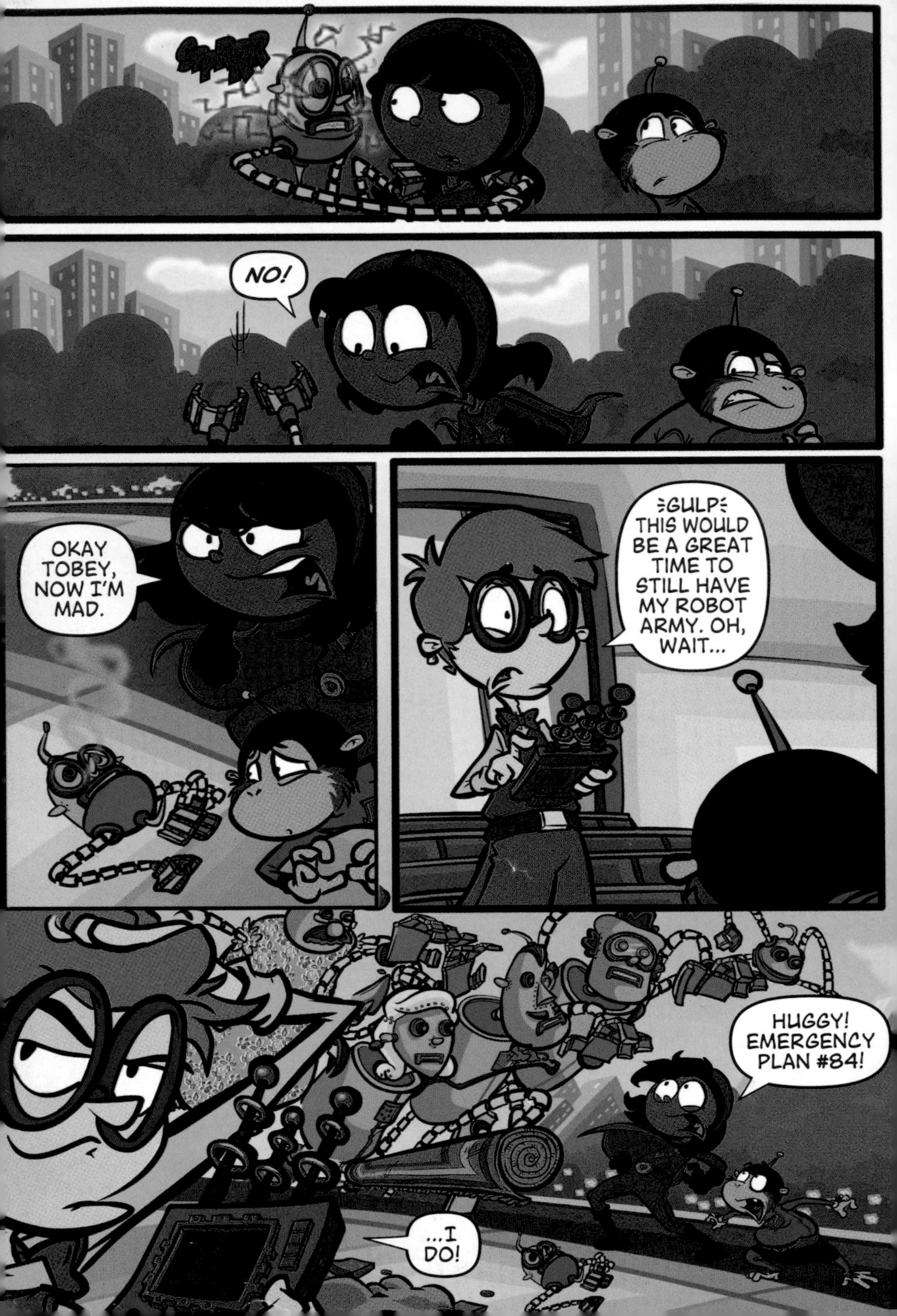
NO!
OKAY TOBEY, NOW I'M MAD.
GULP THIS WOULD BE A GREAT TIME TO STILL HAVE MY ROBOT ARMY. OH, WAIT...
...I DO!
HUGGY! EMERGENCY PLAN #84!

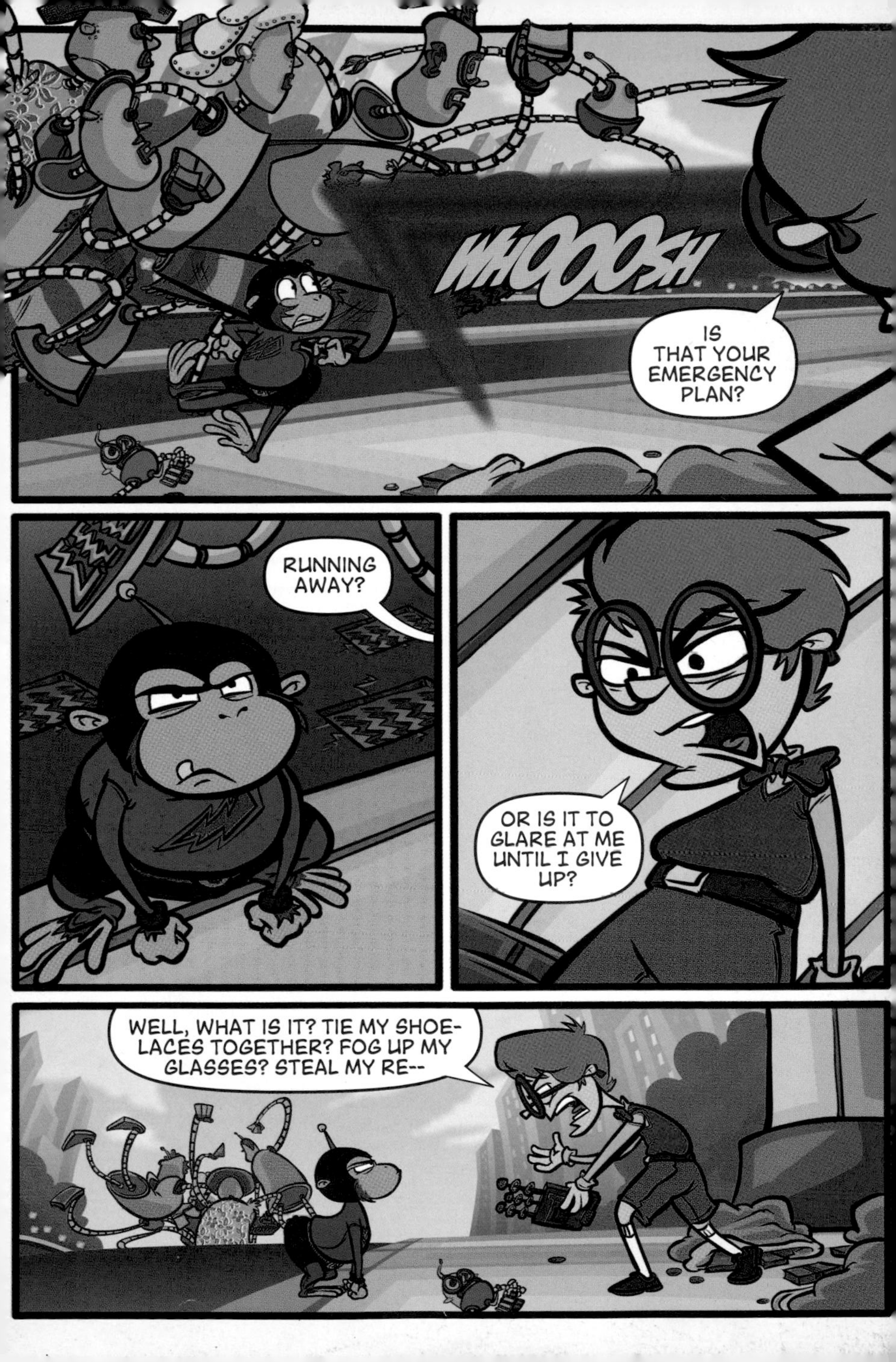
WHOOOOSH
IS THAT YOUR EMERGENCY PLAN?
RUNNING AWAY?
OR IS IT TO GLARE AT ME UNTIL I GIVE UP?
WELL, WHAT IS IT? TIE MY SHOE-LACES TOGETHER? FOG UP MY GLASSES? STEAL MY RE--

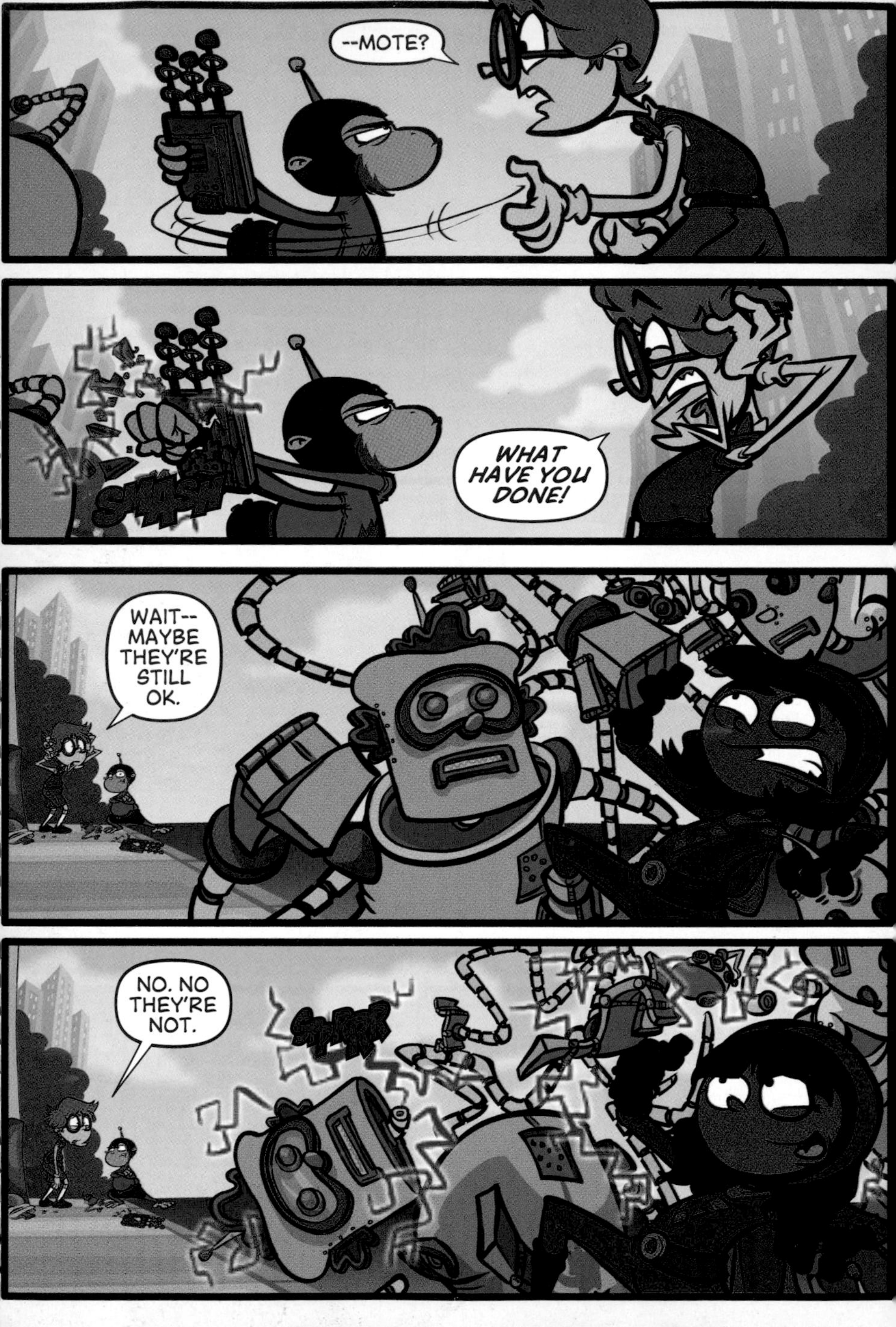
--MOTE?
WHAT HAVE YOU DONE!
WAIT-- MAYBE THEY'RE STILL OK.
NO. NO THEY'RE NOT.

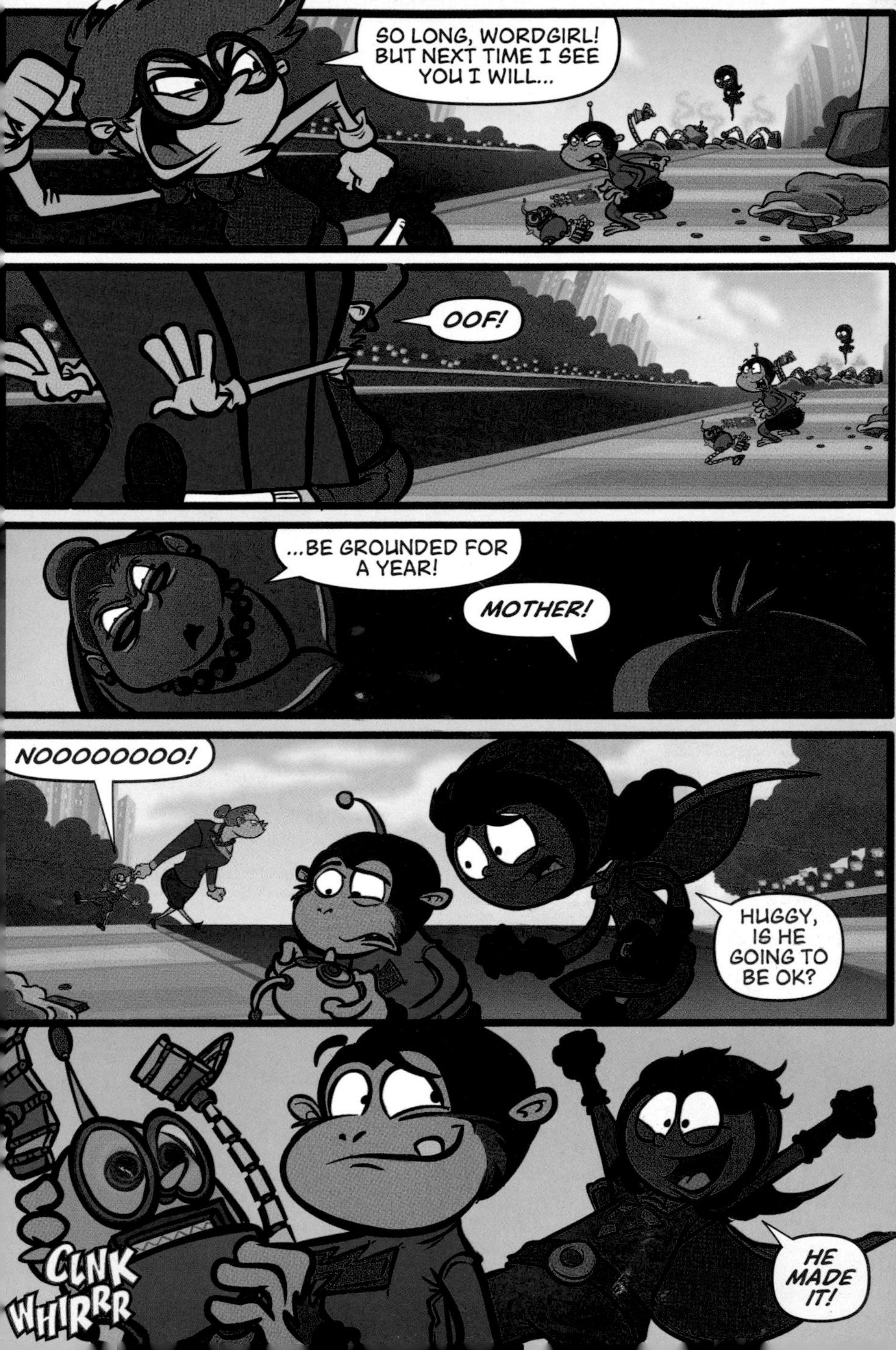
SO LONG, WORDGIRL! BUT NEXT TIME I SEE YOU I WILL...
OOF!
...BE GROUNDED FOR A YEAR!
MOTHER!
NOOOOOOOO!
HUGGY, IS HE GOING TO BE OK?
CLNK
WHIRRR
HE MADE IT!

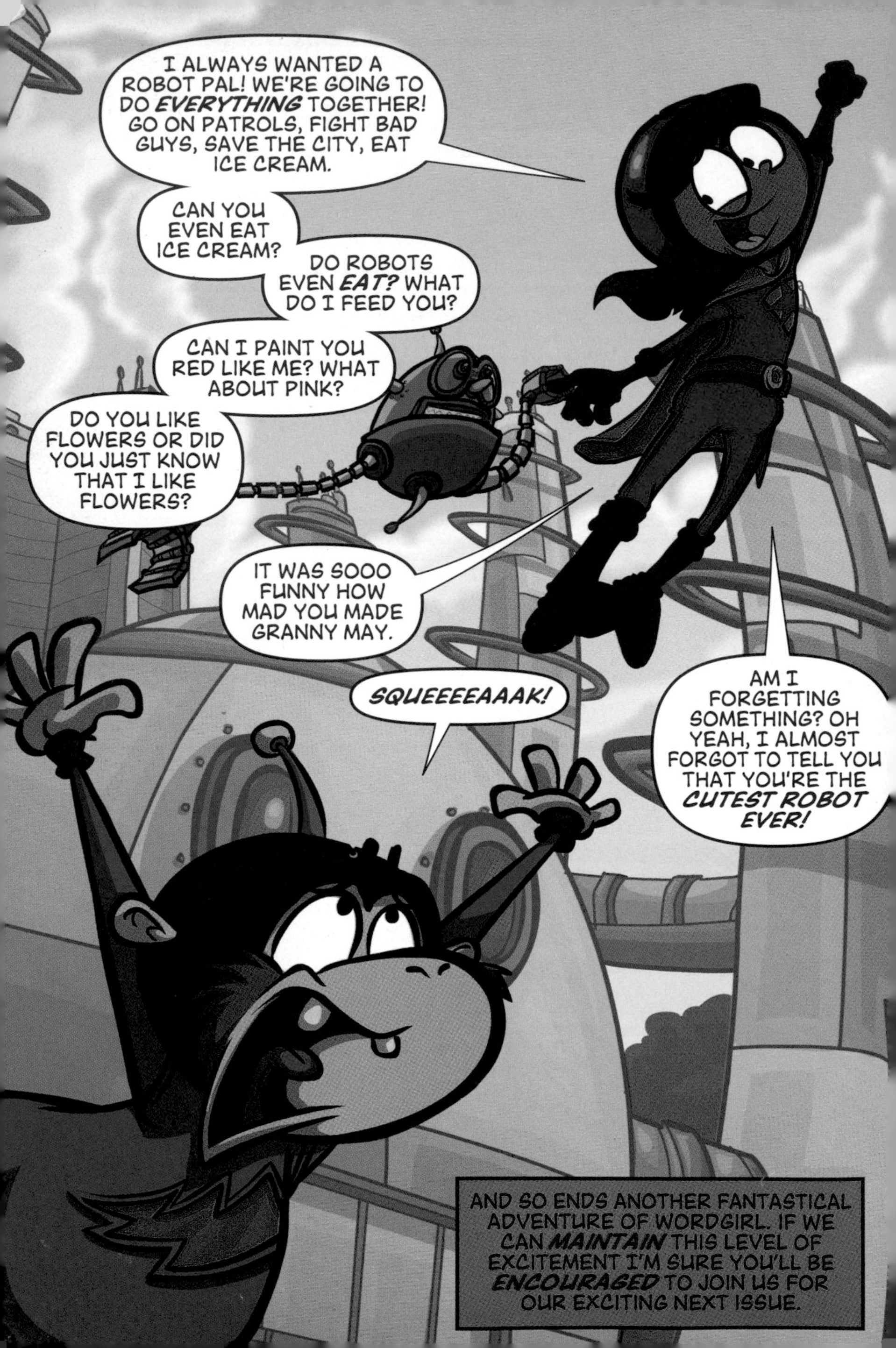
I ALWAYS WANTED A ROBOT PAL! WE'RE GOING TO DO *EVERYTHING* TOGETHER! GO ON PATROLS, FIGHT BAD GUYS, SAVE THE CITY, EAT ICE CREAM.
CAN YOU EVEN EAT ICE CREAM?
DO ROBOTS EVEN *EAT?* WHAT DO I FEED YOU?
CAN I PAINT YOU RED LIKE ME? WHAT ABOUT PINK?
DO YOU LIKE FLOWERS OR DID YOU JUST KNOW THAT I LIKE FLOWERS?
IT WAS SOOO FUNNY HOW MAD YOU MADE GRANNY MAY.
SQUEEEEAAAK!
AM I FORGETTING SOMETHING? OH YEAH, I ALMOST FORGOT TO TELL YOU THAT YOU'RE THE *CUTEST ROBOT EVER!*
AND SO ENDS ANOTHER FANTASTICAL ADVENTURE OF WORDGIRL. IF WE CAN *MAINTAIN* THIS LEVEL OF EXCITEMENT I'M SURE YOU'LL BE *ENCOURAGED* TO JOIN US FOR OUR EXCITING NEXT ISSUE.

FONDUE, FONDON'T

Anita Serwacki
WRITER

Andy Price
ART

Dustin Evans
COLORS

Steve Wands
LETTERS

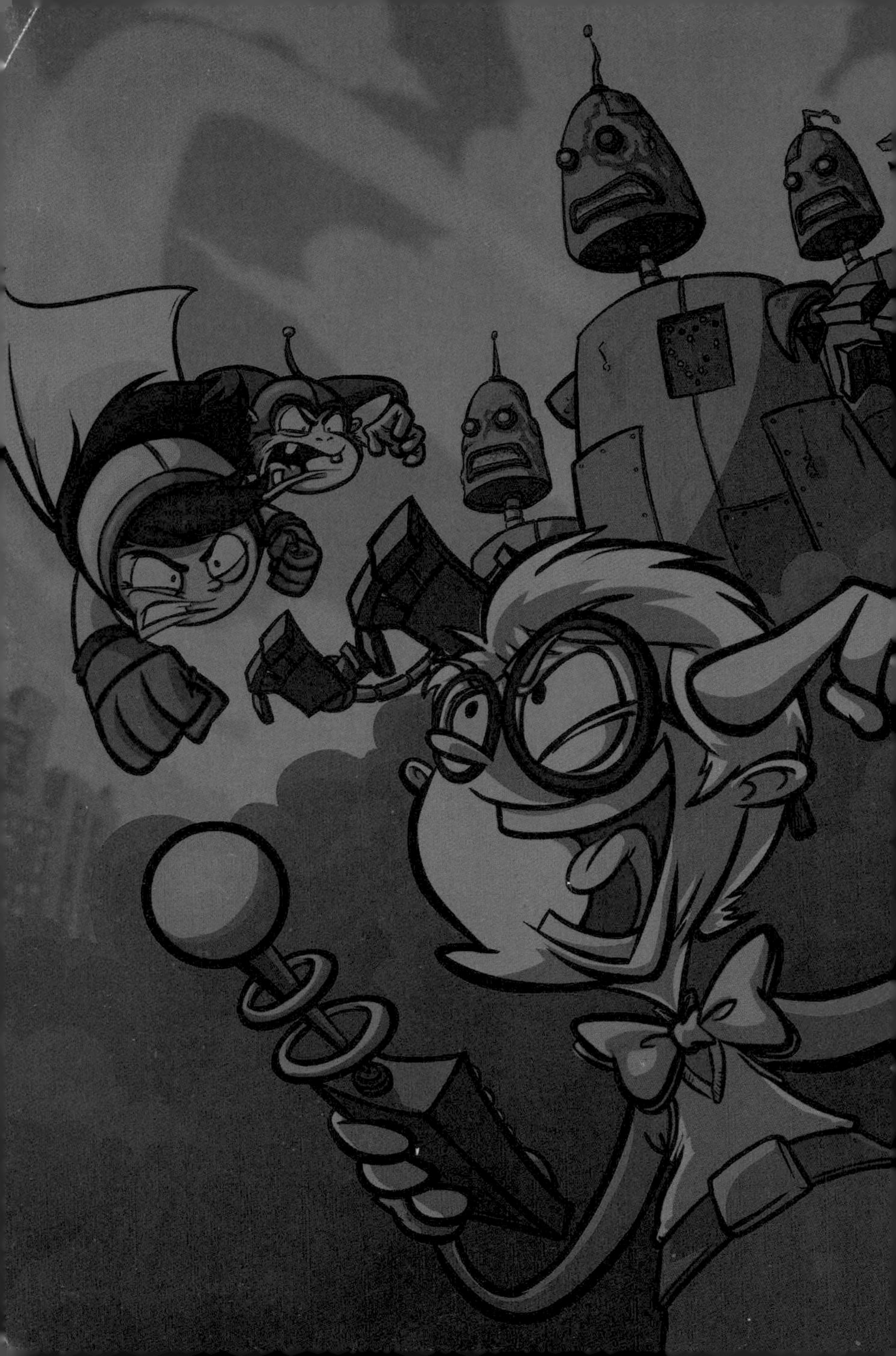

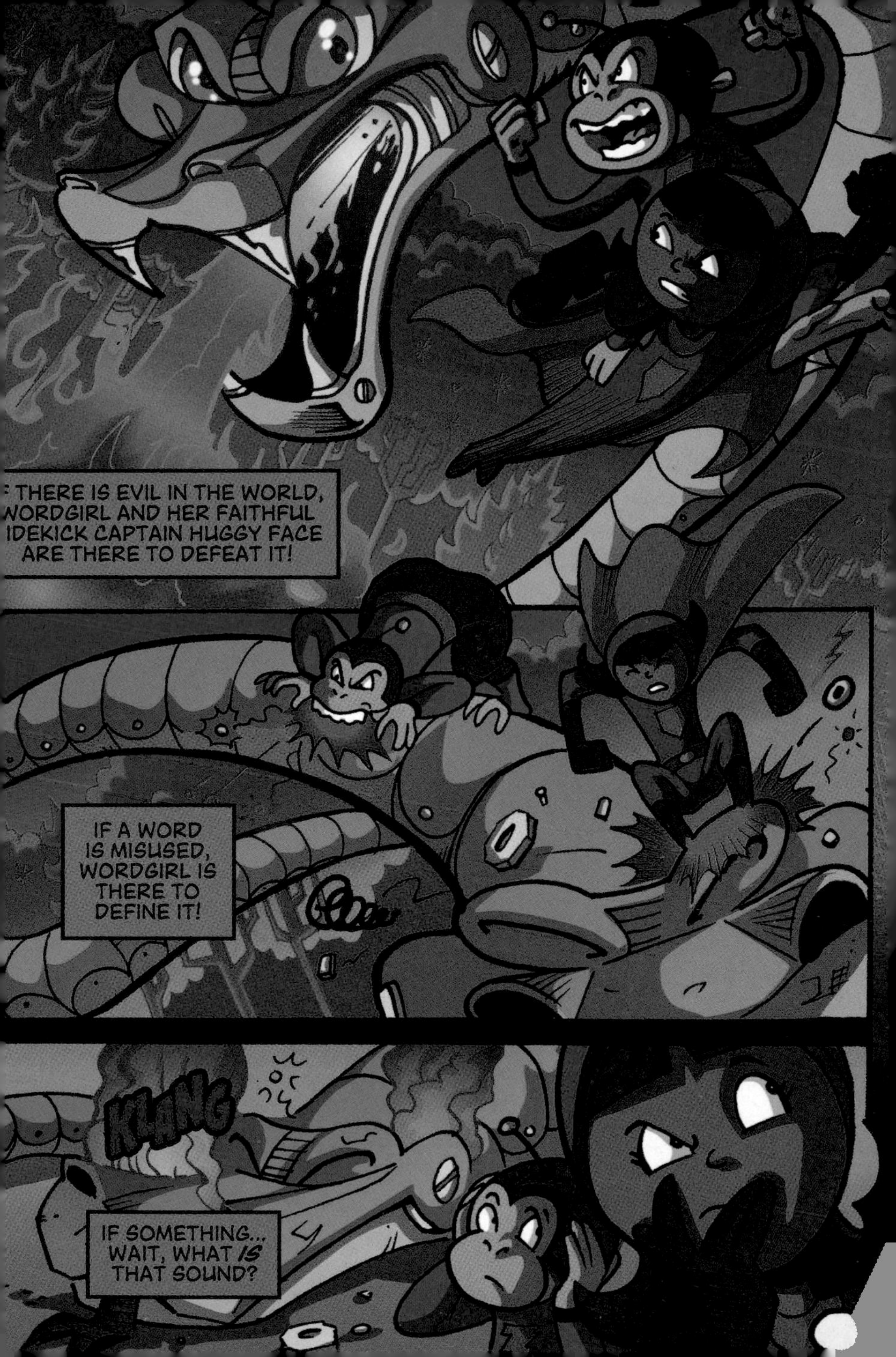

F THERE IS EVIL IN THE WORLD, WORDGIRL AND HER FAITHFUL IDEKICK CAPTAIN HUGGY FACE ARE THERE TO DEFEAT IT!
IF A WORD IS MISUSED, WORDGIRL IS THERE TO DEFINE IT!
KLANG
IF SOMETHING... WAIT, WHAT *IS* THAT SOUND?

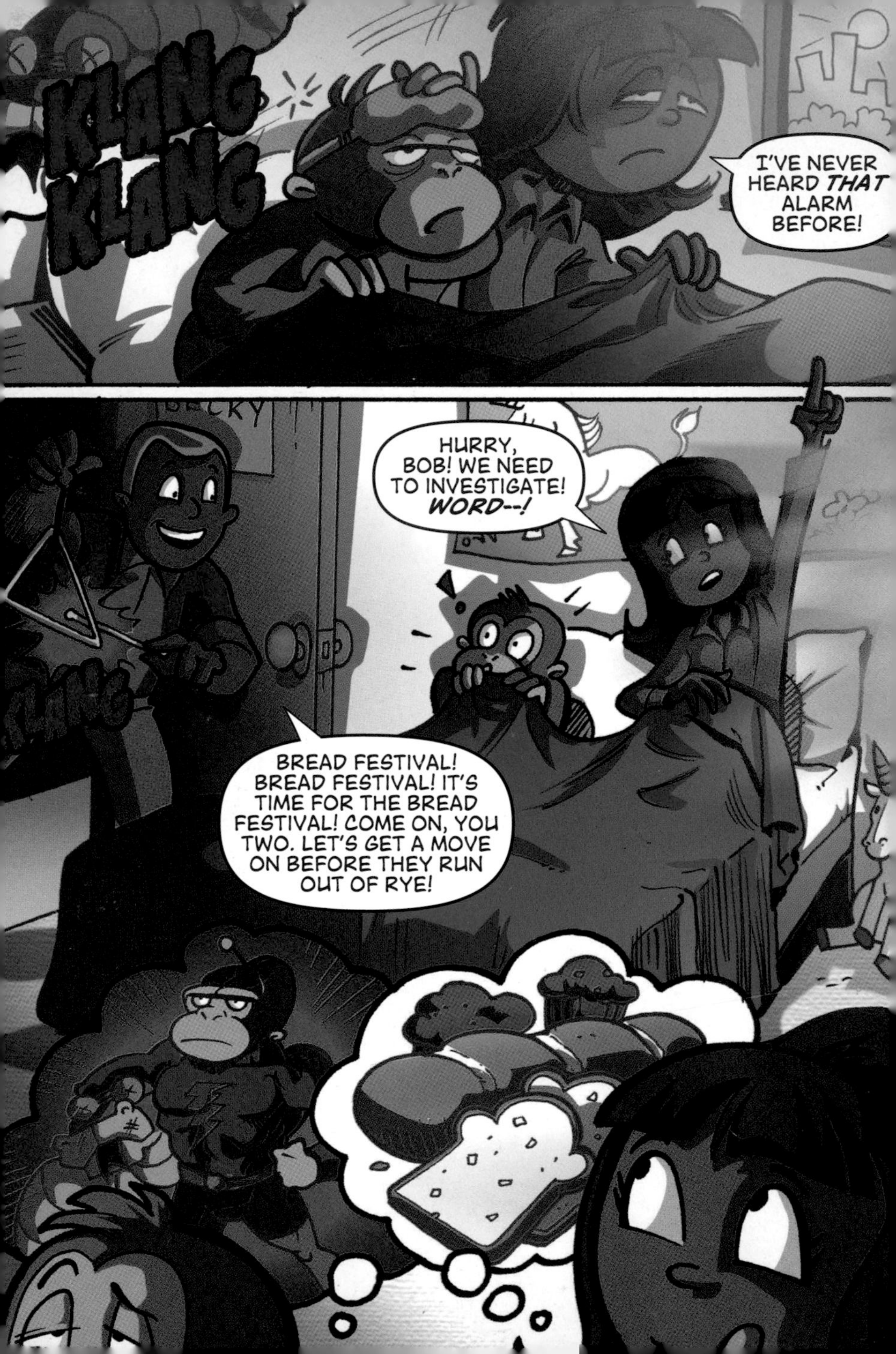

KLANG KLANG
I'VE NEVER HEARD *THAT* ALARM BEFORE!
BECKY
HURRY, BOB! WE NEED TO INVESTIGATE! *WORD--!*
KLANG
BREAD FESTIVAL! BREAD FESTIVAL! IT'S TIME FOR THE BREAD FESTIVAL! COME ON, YOU TWO. LET'S GET A MOVE ON BEFORE THEY RUN OUT OF RYE!

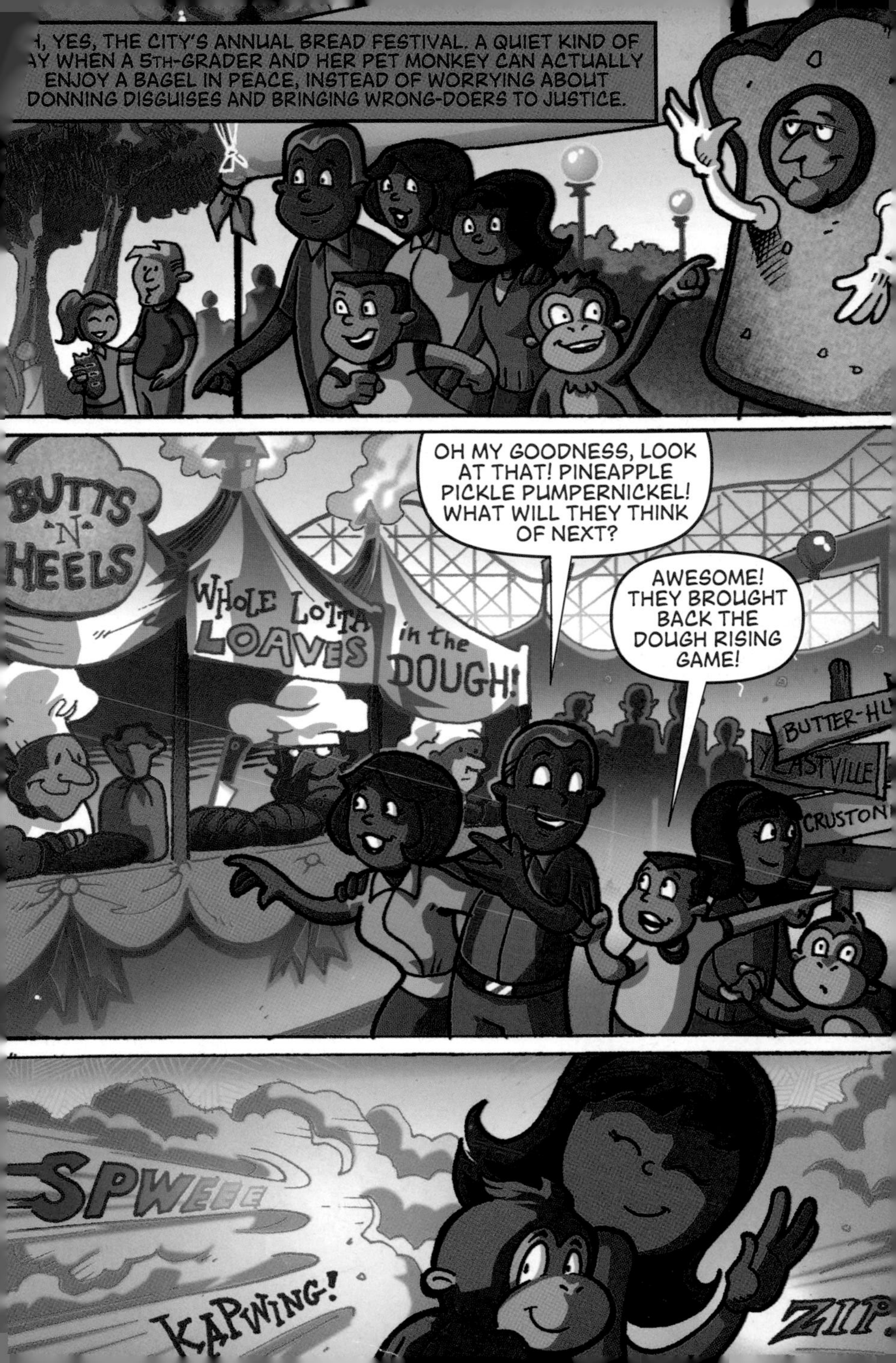
H, YES, THE CITY'S ANNUAL BREAD FESTIVAL. A QUIET KIND OF AY WHEN A 5TH-GRADER AND HER PET MONKEY CAN ACTUALLY ENJOY A BAGEL IN PEACE, INSTEAD OF WORRYING ABOUT DONNING DISGUISES AND BRINGING WRONG-DOERS TO JUSTICE.
BUTTS 'N' HEELS
WHOLE LOTTA LOAVES
in the DOUGH!
OH MY GOODNESS, LOOK AT THAT! PINEAPPLE PICKLE PUMPERNICKEL! WHAT WILL THEY THINK OF NEXT?
AWESOME! THEY BROUGHT BACK THE DOUGH RISING GAME!
BUTTER-H
YEASTVILLE
CRUSTON
SPWEEE
KAPWING!
ZIP!

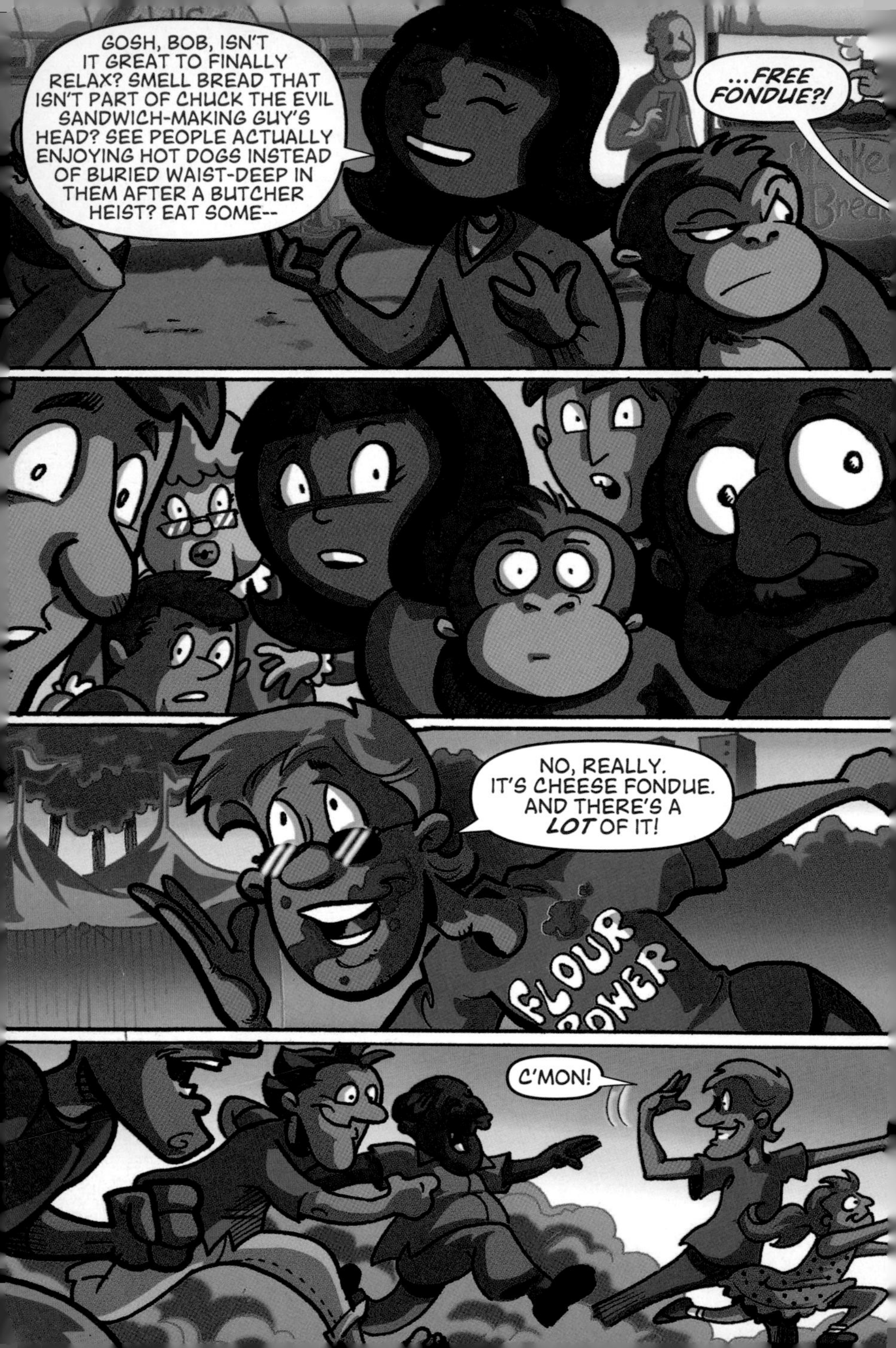
GOSH, BOB, ISN'T IT GREAT TO FINALLY RELAX? SMELL BREAD THAT ISN'T PART OF CHUCK THE EVIL SANDWICH-MAKING GUY'S HEAD? SEE PEOPLE ACTUALLY ENJOYING HOT DOGS INSTEAD OF BURIED WAIST-DEEP IN THEM AFTER A BUTCHER HEIST? EAT SOME--
...FREE FONDUE?!
NO, REALLY. IT'S CHEESE FONDUE. AND THERE'S A LOT OF IT!
FLOUR POWER
C'MON!

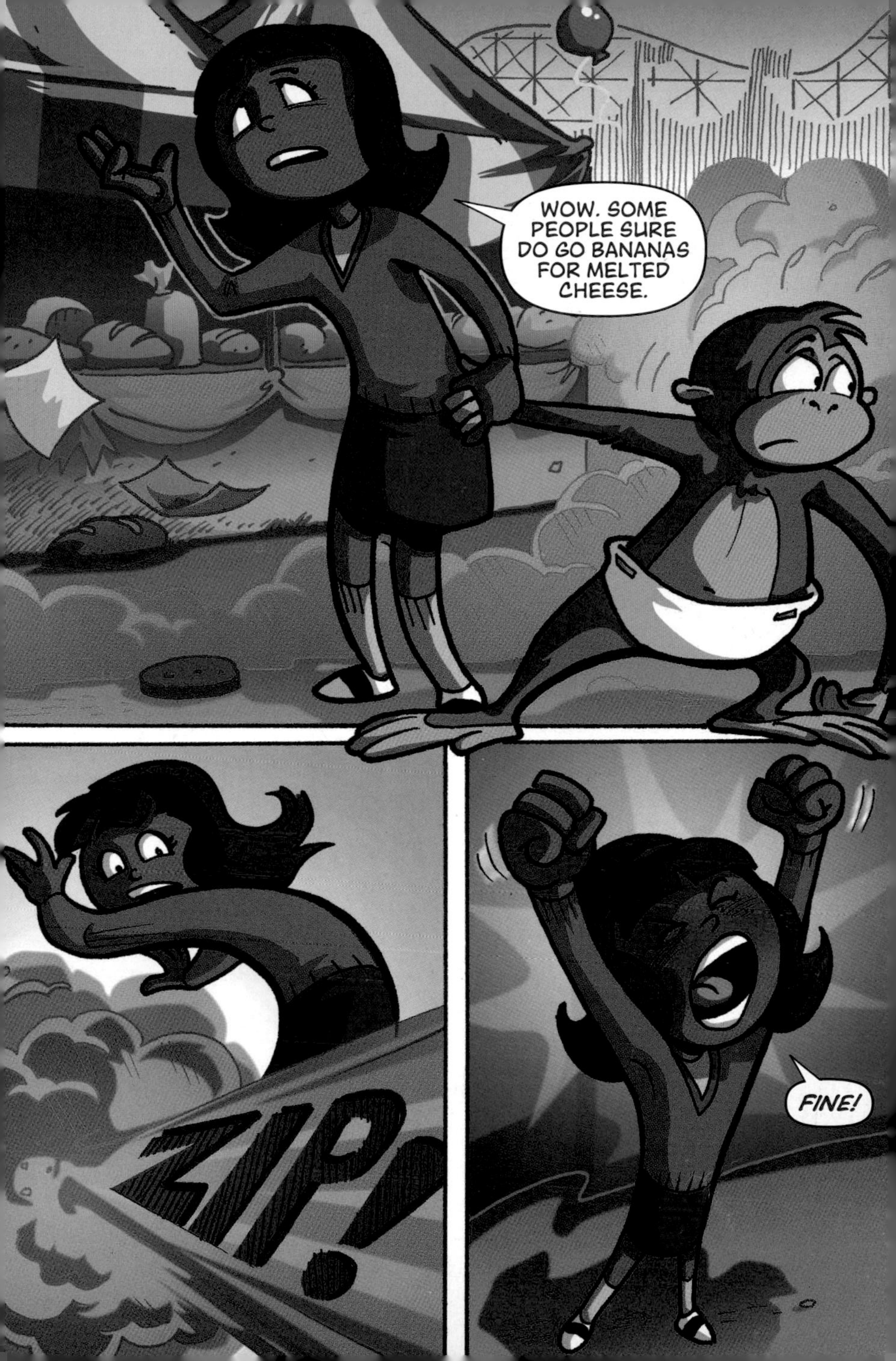
WOW. SOME PEOPLE SURE DO GO BANANAS FOR MELTED CHEESE.
ZIP!
FINE!

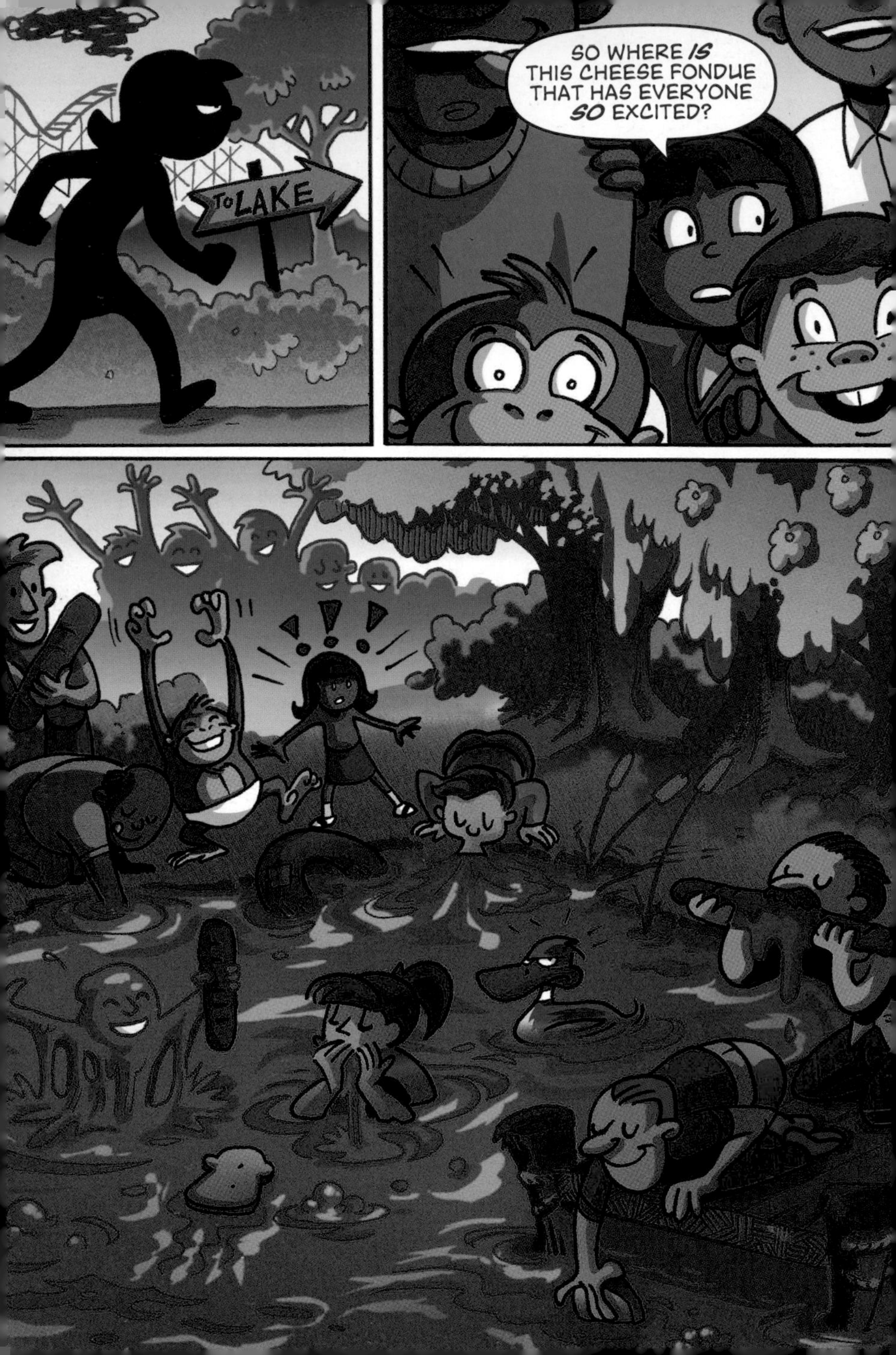
TO LAKE
SO WHERE IS THIS CHEESE FONDUE THAT HAS EVERYONE SO EXCITED?

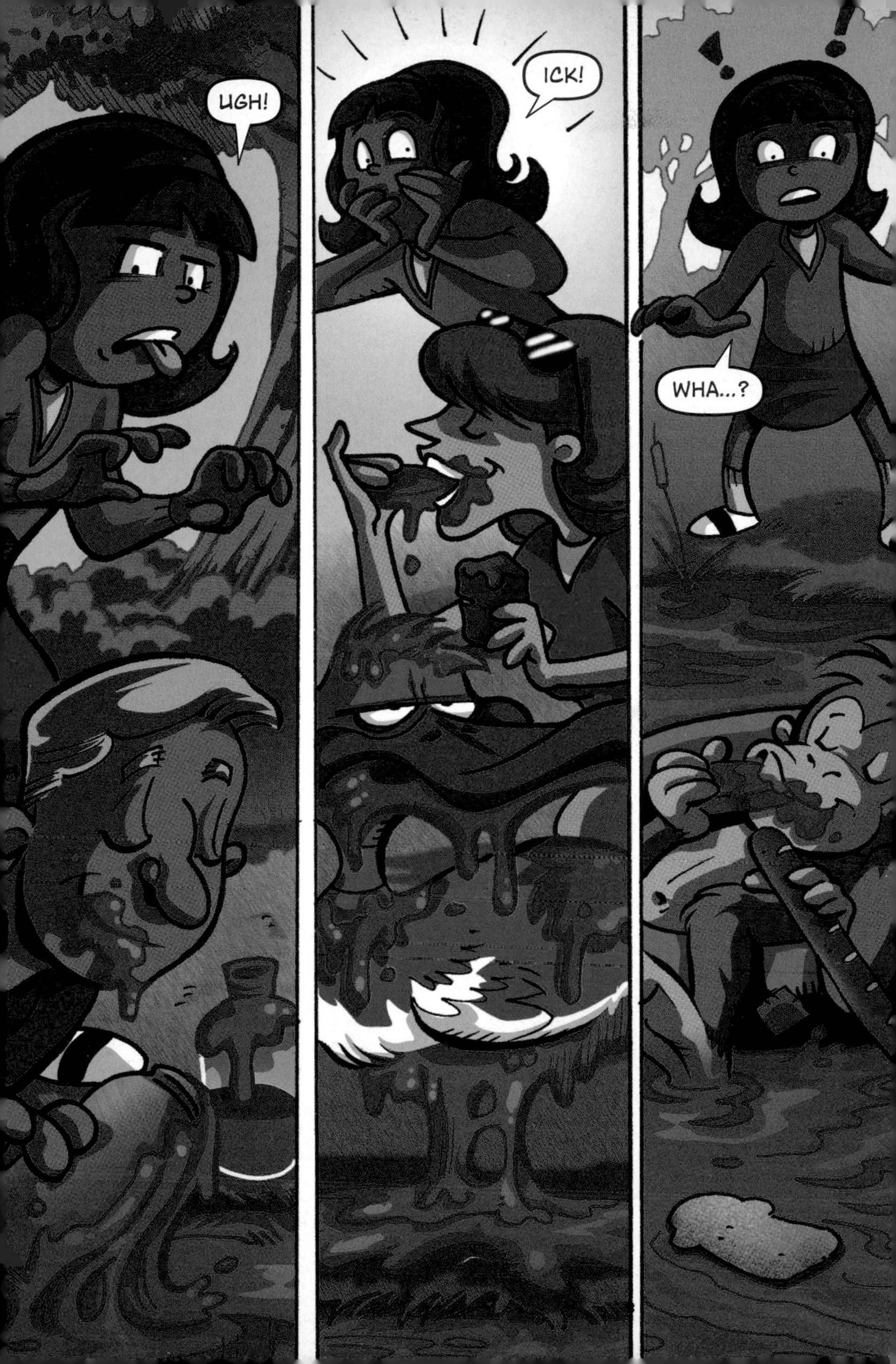
UGH!
ICK!
WHA...?

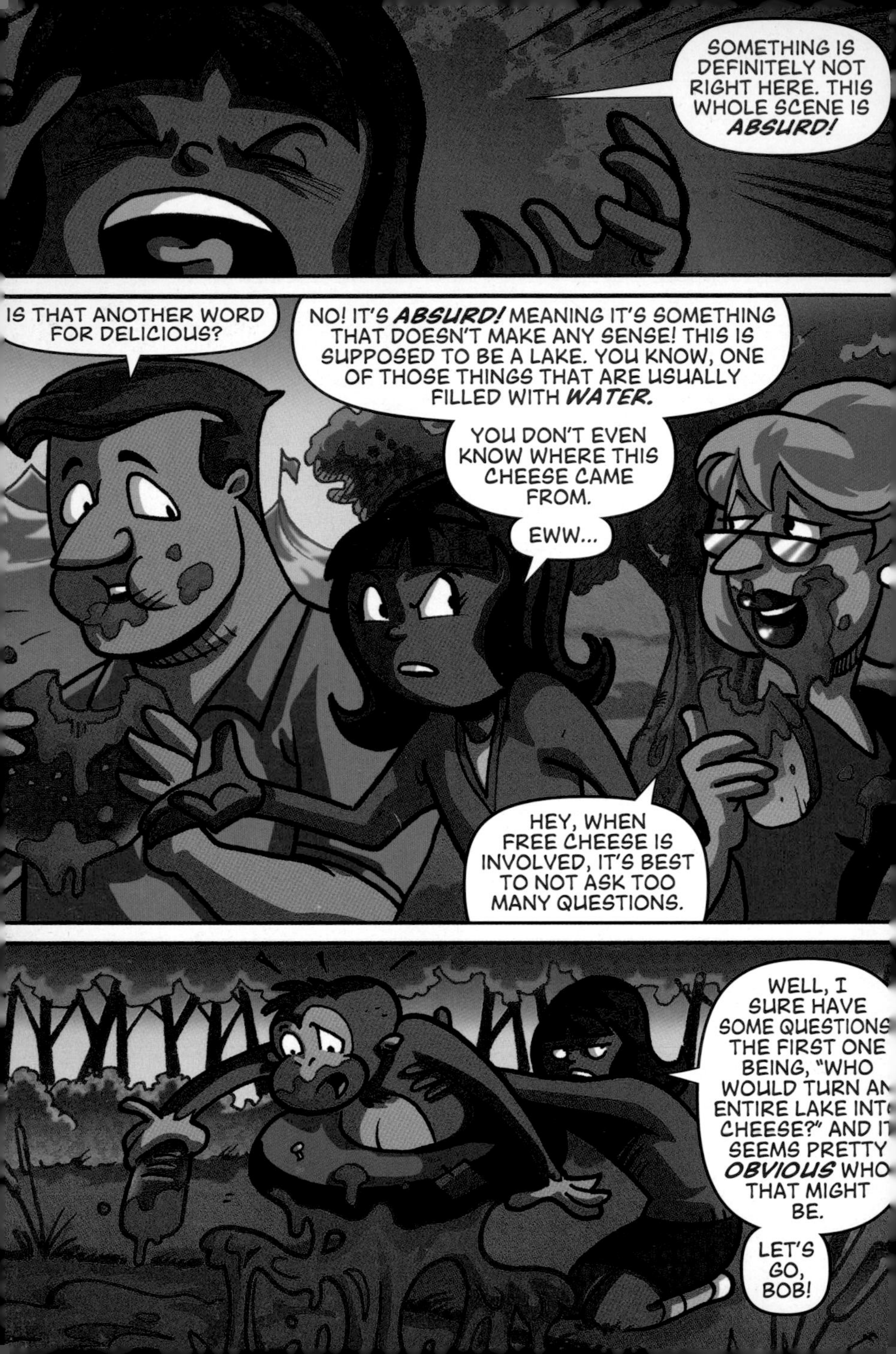
SOMETHING IS DEFINITELY NOT RIGHT HERE. THIS WHOLE SCENE IS *ABSURD!*
IS THAT ANOTHER WORD FOR DELICIOUS?
NO! IT'S *ABSURD!* MEANING IT'S SOMETHING THAT DOESN'T MAKE ANY SENSE! THIS IS SUPPOSED TO BE A LAKE. YOU KNOW, ONE OF THOSE THINGS THAT ARE USUALLY FILLED WITH *WATER.*
YOU DON'T EVEN KNOW WHERE THIS CHEESE CAME FROM.
EWW...
HEY, WHEN FREE CHEESE IS INVOLVED, IT'S BEST TO NOT ASK TOO MANY QUESTIONS.
WELL, I SURE HAVE SOME QUESTIONS THE FIRST ONE BEING, "WHO WOULD TURN AN ENTIRE LAKE INTO CHEESE?" AND IT SEEMS PRETTY *OBVIOUS* WHO THAT MIGHT BE.
LET'S GO, BOB!

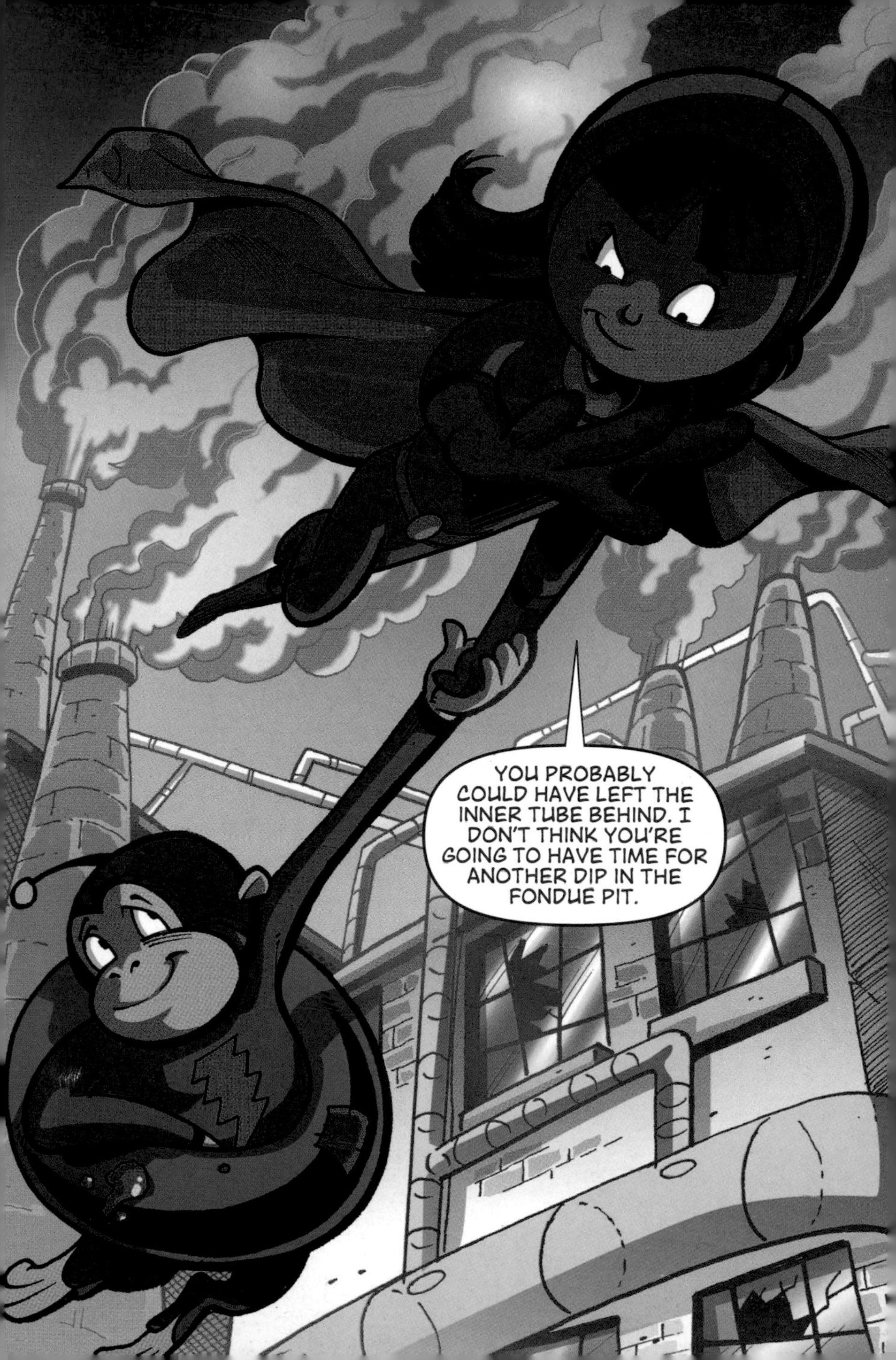
YOU PROBABLY COULD HAVE LEFT THE INNER TUBE BEHIND. I DON'T THINK YOU'RE GOING TO HAVE TIME FOR ANOTHER DIP IN THE FONDUE PIT.

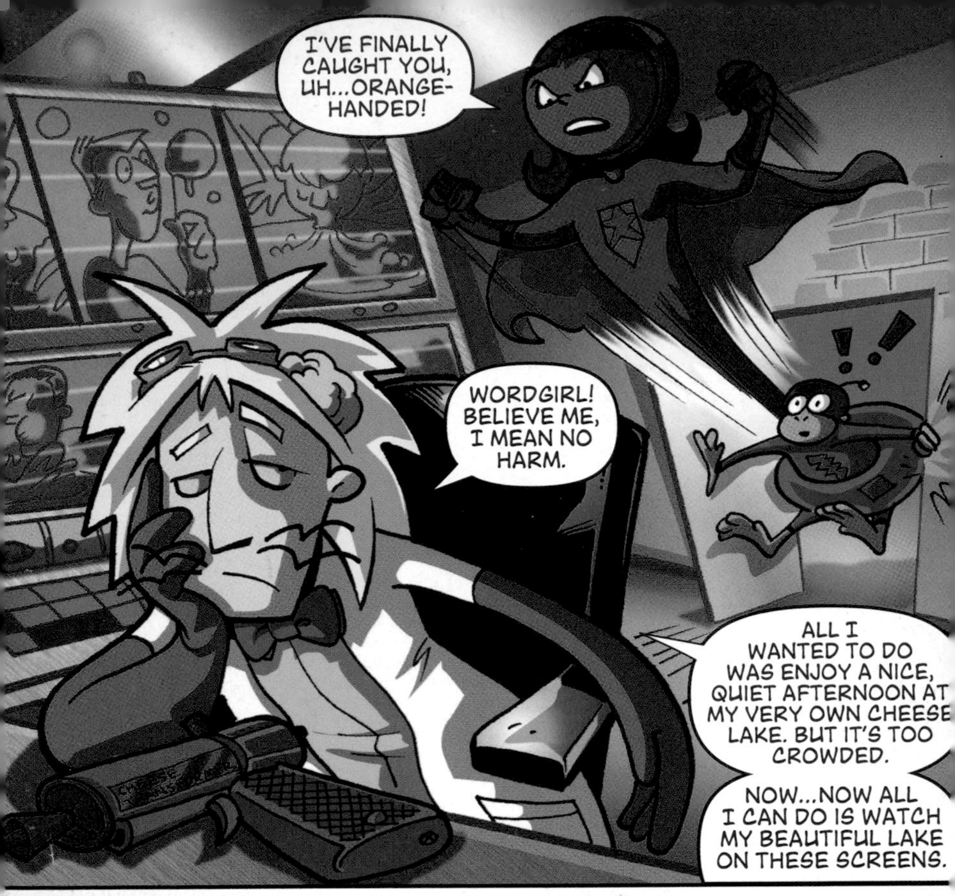
I'VE FINALLY CAUGHT YOU, UH...ORANGE-HANDED!
WORDGIRL! BELIEVE ME, I MEAN NO HARM.
ALL I WANTED TO DO WAS ENJOY A NICE, QUIET AFTERNOON AT MY VERY OWN CHEESE LAKE. BUT IT'S TOO CROWDED.
NOW...NOW ALL I CAN DO IS WATCH MY BEAUTIFUL LAKE ON THESE SCREENS.

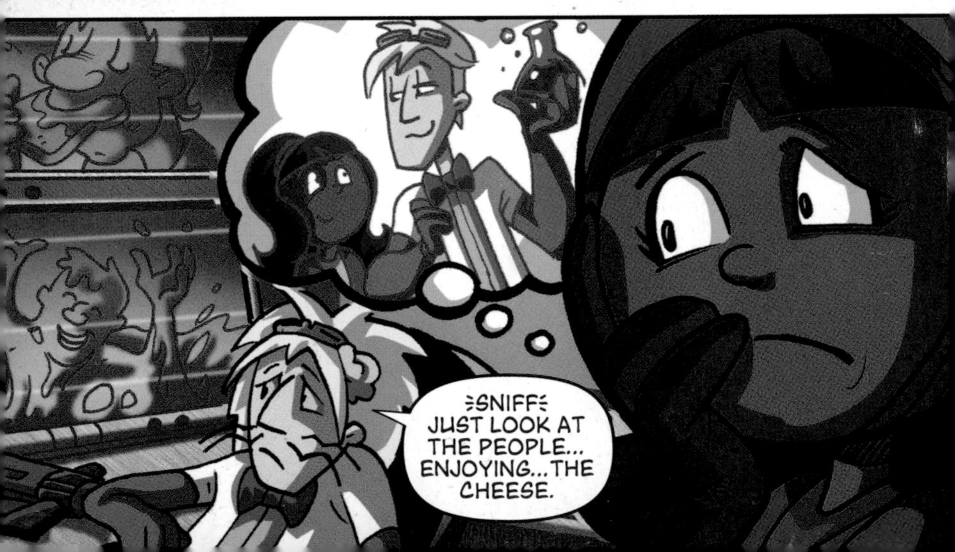
SNIFF
JUST LOOK AT THE PEOPLE... ENJOYING...THE CHEESE.

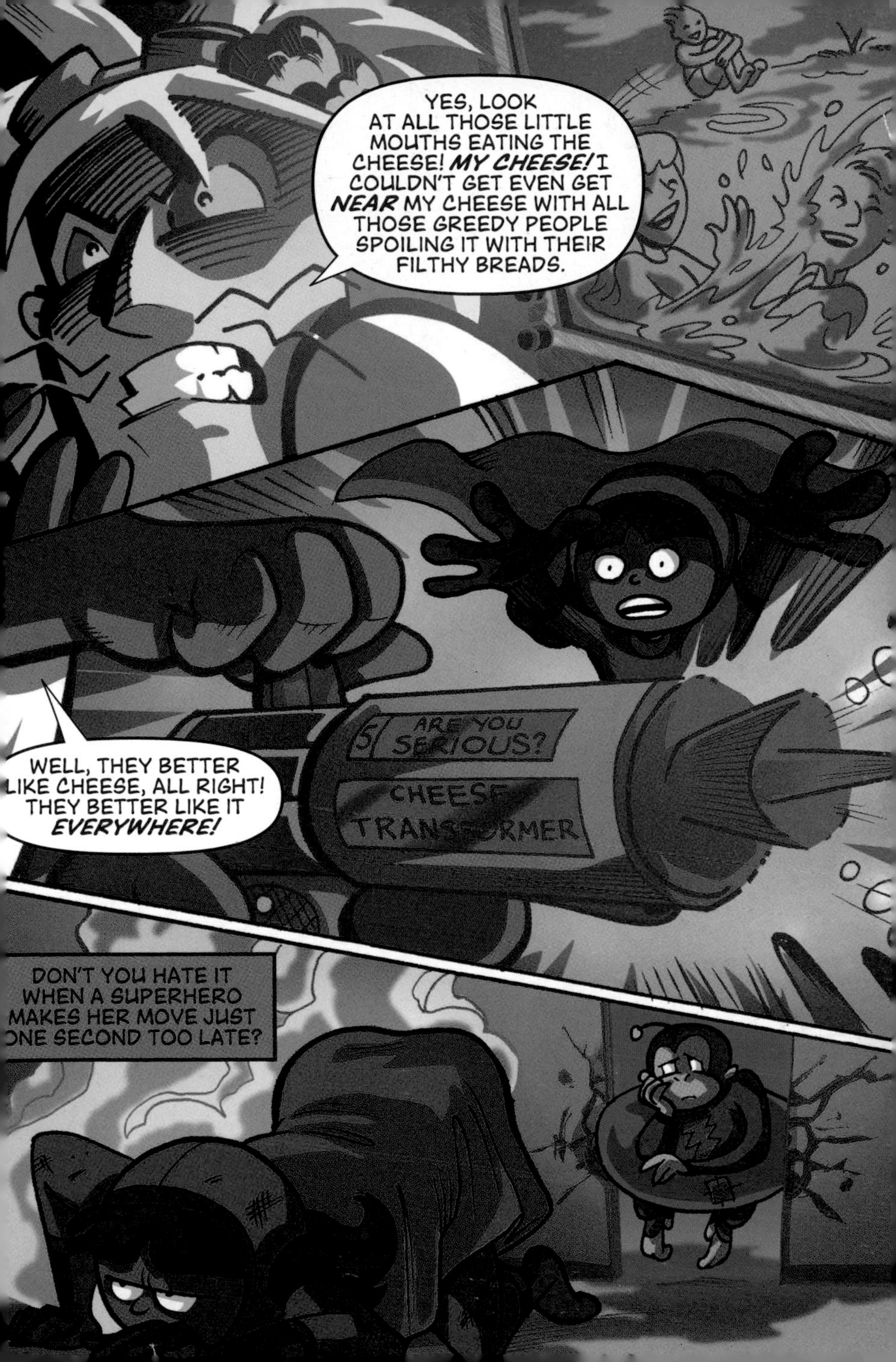
YES, LOOK AT ALL THOSE LITTLE MOUTHS EATING THE CHEESE! **MY CHEESE!** I COULDN'T GET EVEN GET **NEAR** MY CHEESE WITH ALL THOSE GREEDY PEOPLE SPOILING IT WITH THEIR FILTHY BREADS.
WELL, THEY BETTER LIKE CHEESE, ALL RIGHT! THEY BETTER LIKE IT **EVERYWHERE!**
5 ARE YOU SERIOUS?
DON'T YOU HATE IT WHEN A SUPERHERO MAKES HER MOVE JUST ONE SECOND TOO LATE?

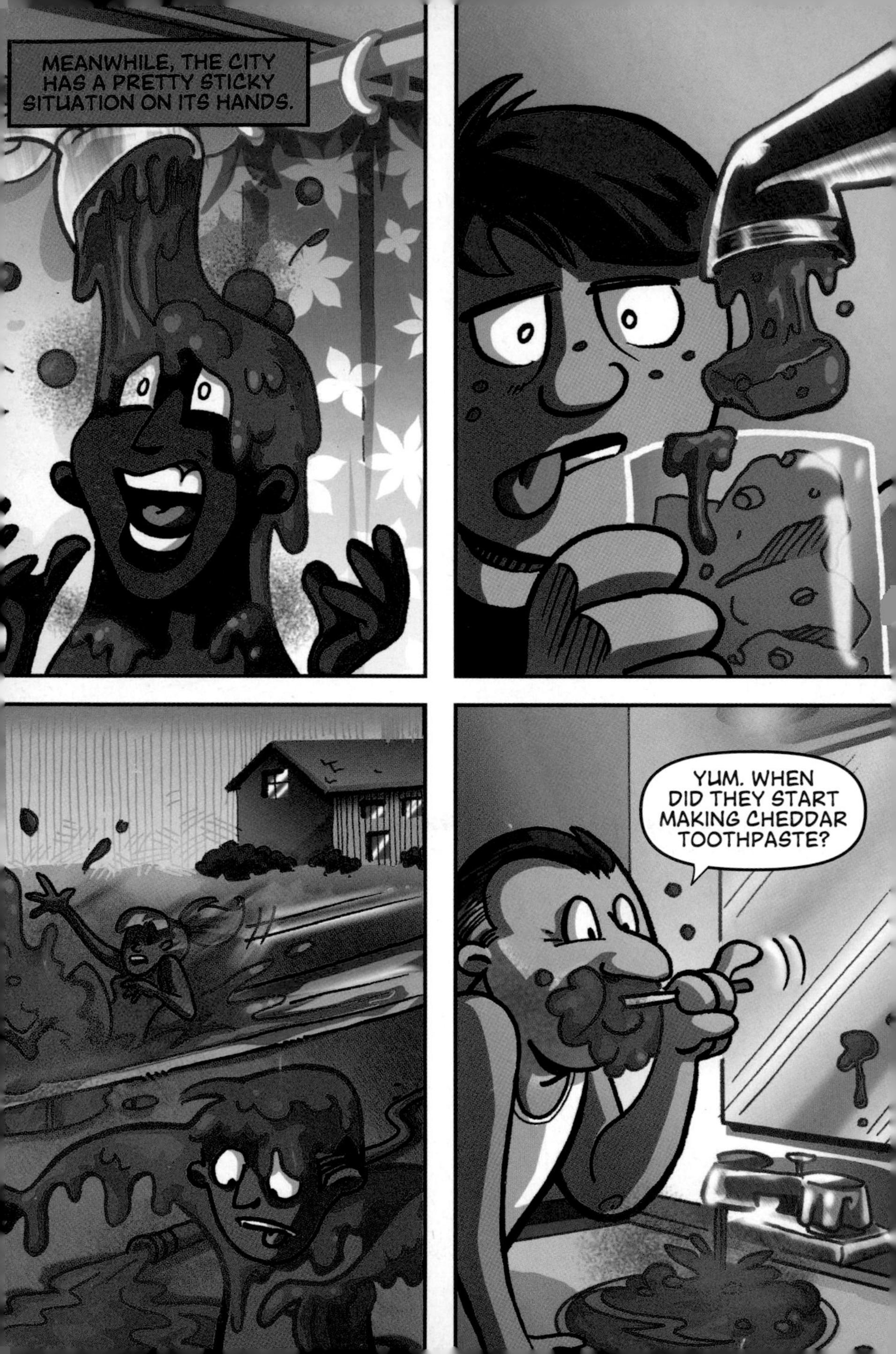
MEANWHILE, THE CITY HAS A PRETTY STICKY SITUATION ON ITS HANDS.
YUM. WHEN DID THEY START MAKING CHEDDAR TOOTHPASTE?

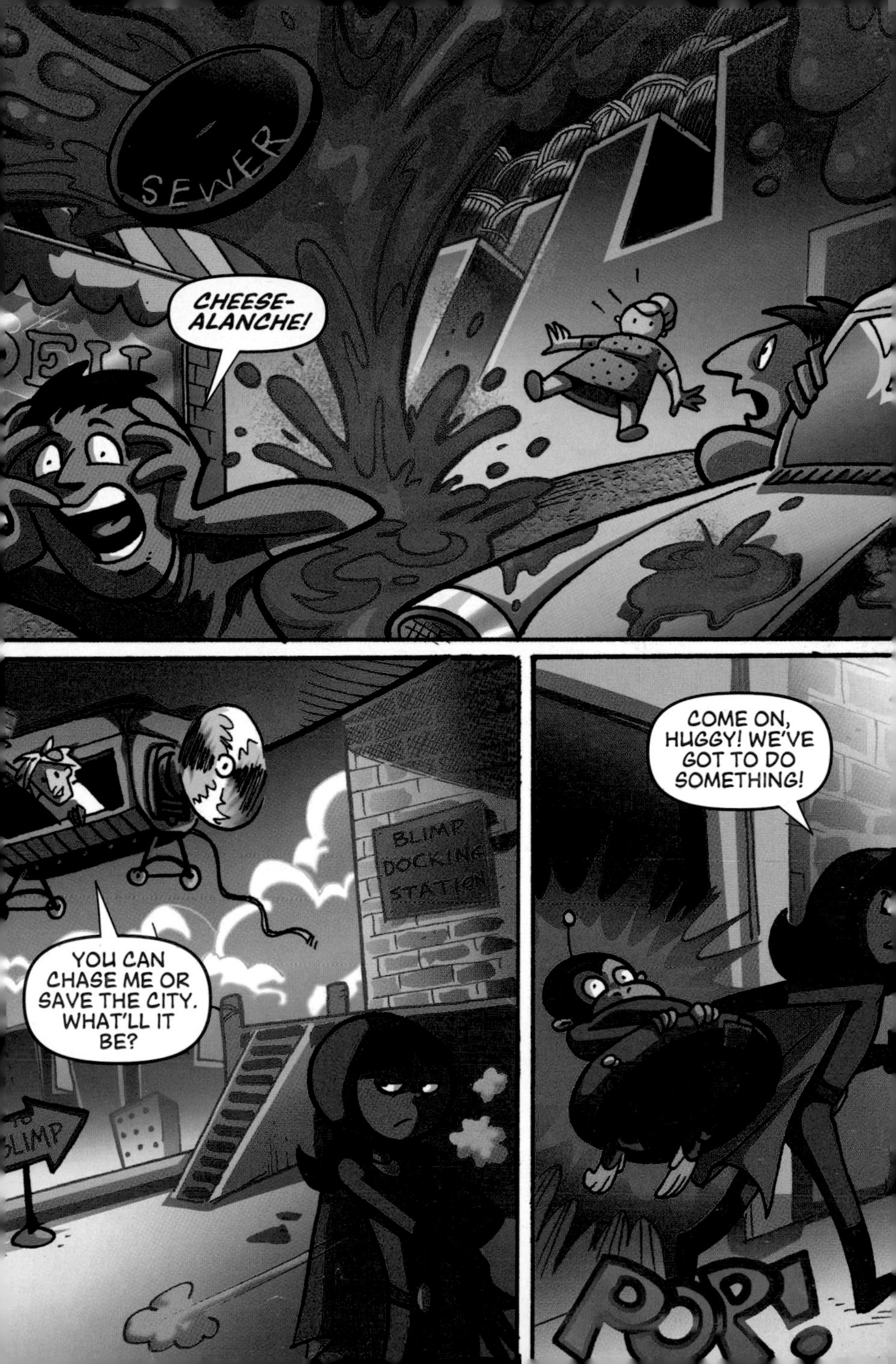
SEWER
CHEESE-ALANCHE!
BLIMP DOCKING STATION
YOU CAN CHASE ME OR SAVE THE CITY. WHAT'LL IT BE?
TO BLIMP
COME ON, HUGGY! WE'VE GOT TO DO SOMETHING!
POP!

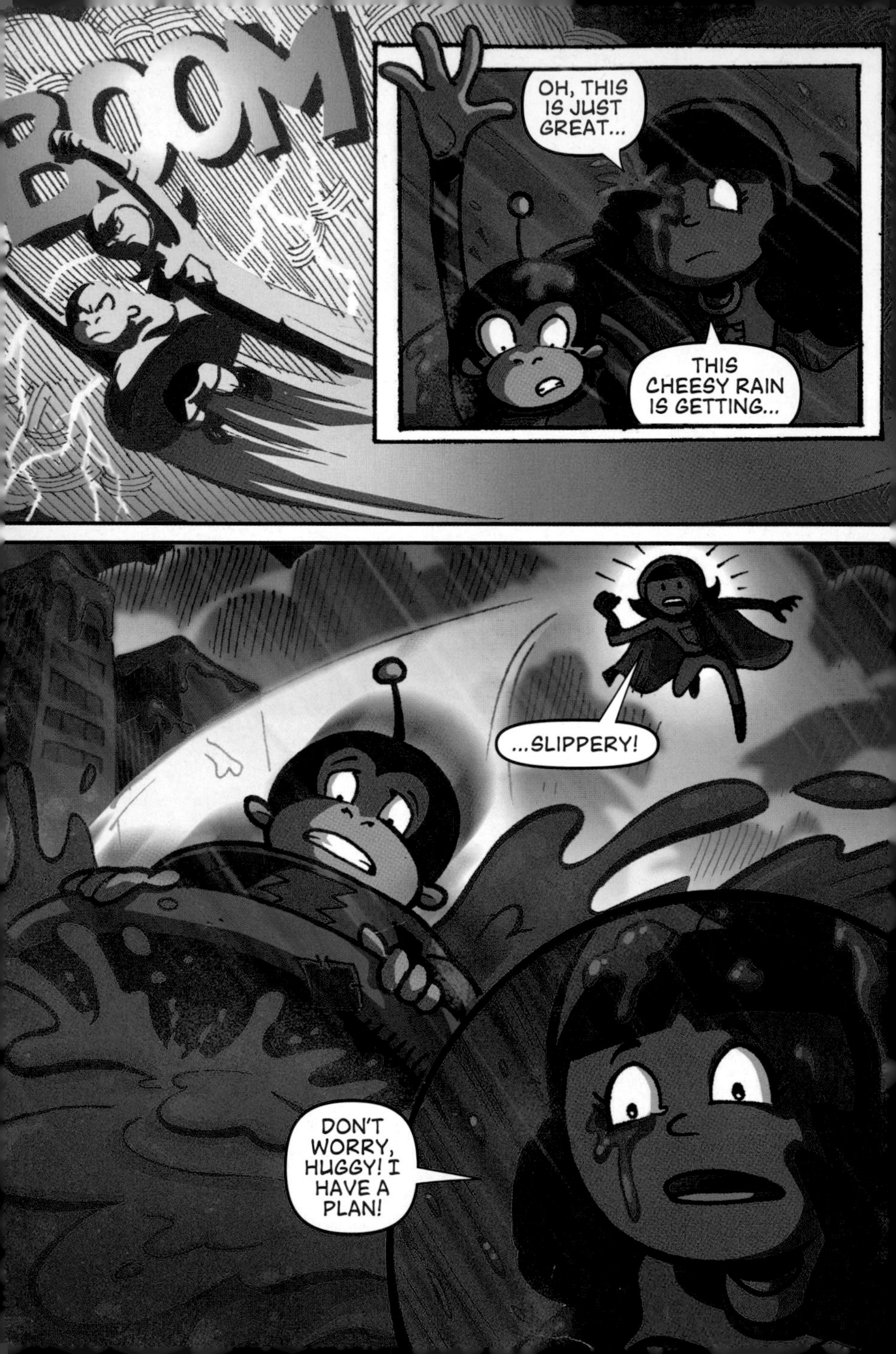
BOOM
OH, THIS IS JUST GREAT...
THIS CHEESY RAIN IS GETTING...
...SLIPPERY!
DON'T WORRY, HUGGY! I HAVE A PLAN!

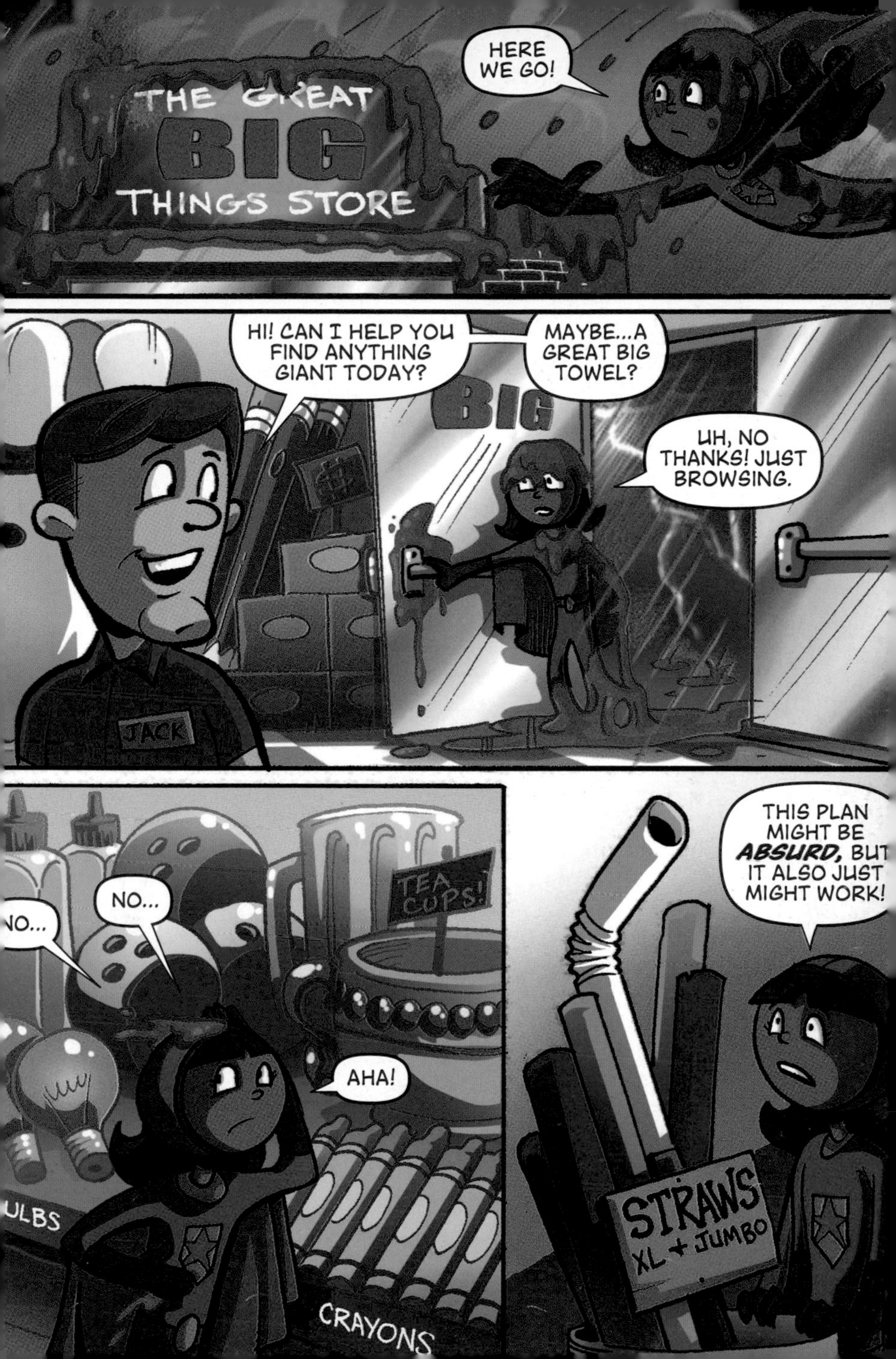
THE GREAT BIG THINGS STORE
HERE WE GO!
HI! CAN I HELP YOU FIND ANYTHING GIANT TODAY?
MAYBE...A GREAT BIG TOWEL?
BIG
UH, NO THANKS! JUST BROWSING.
JACK
NO...
NO...
TEA CUPS!
AHA!
ULBS
CRAYONS
THIS PLAN MIGHT BE ***ABSURD,*** BUT IT ALSO JUST MIGHT WORK!
STRAWS XL + JUMBO

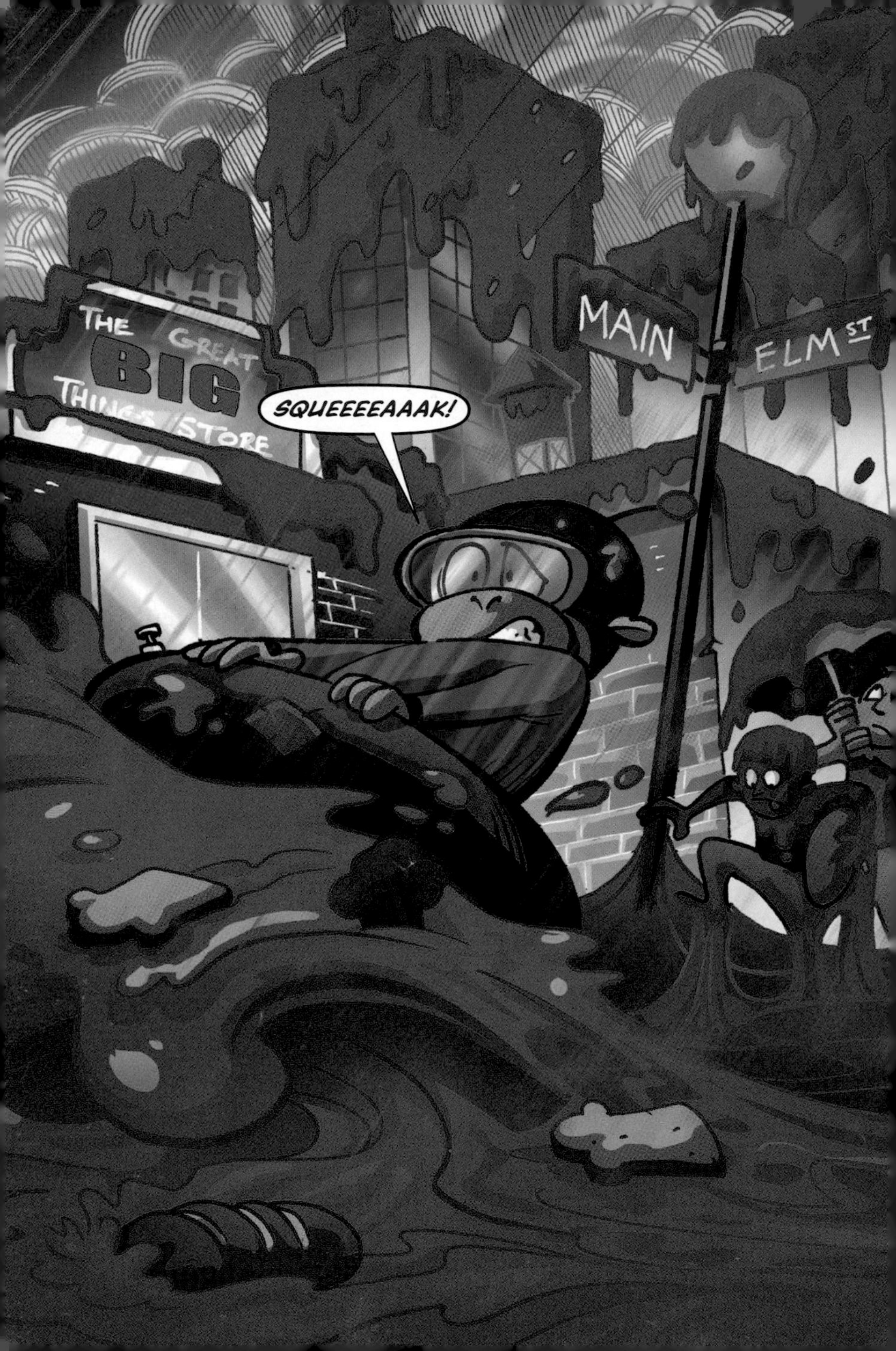
THE GREAT BIG THINGS STORE
SQUEEEEEAAAK!
MAIN
ELM ST

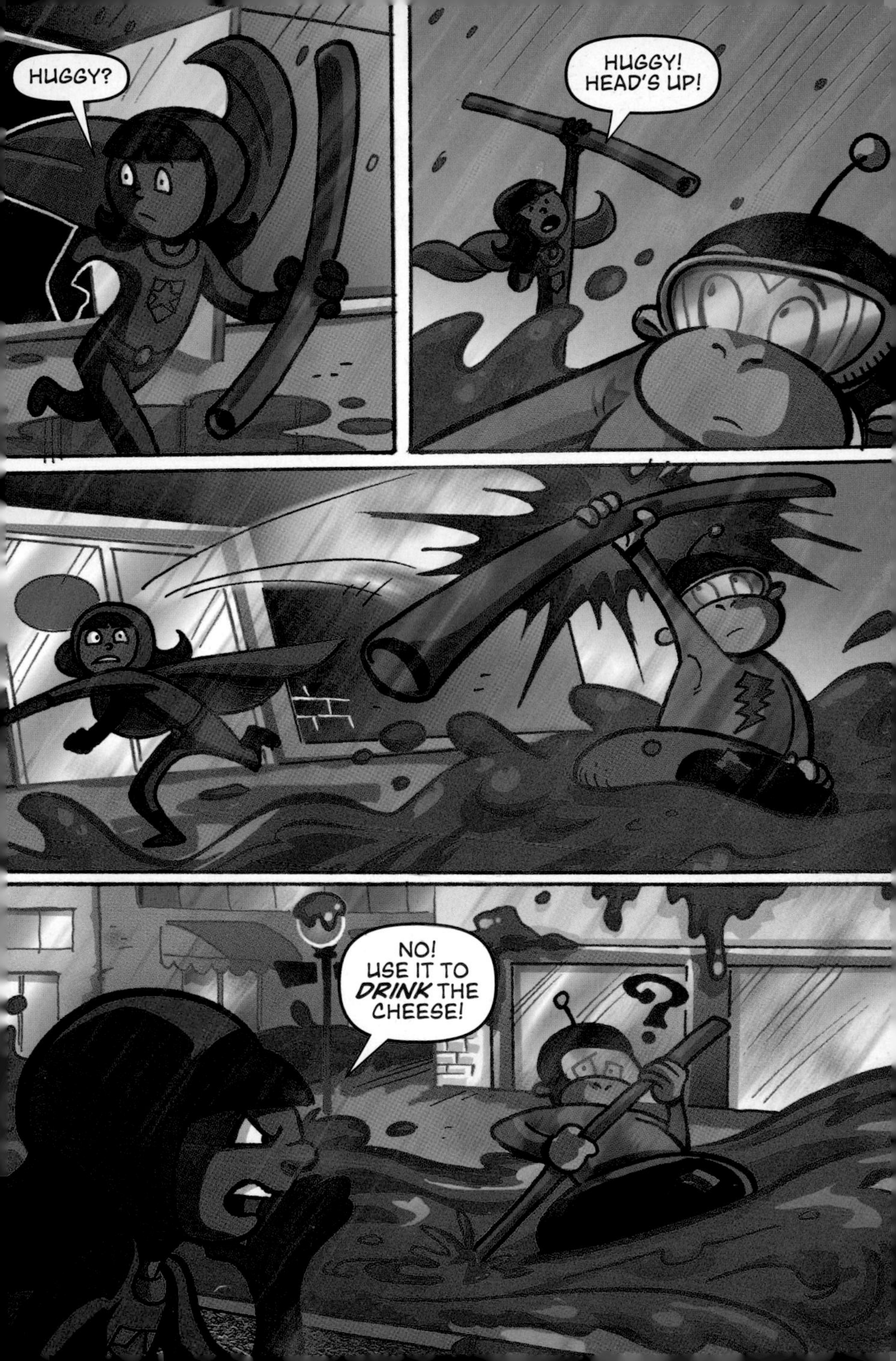
HUGGY?
HUGGY! HEAD'S UP!
NO! USE IT TO *DRINK* THE CHEESE!
?

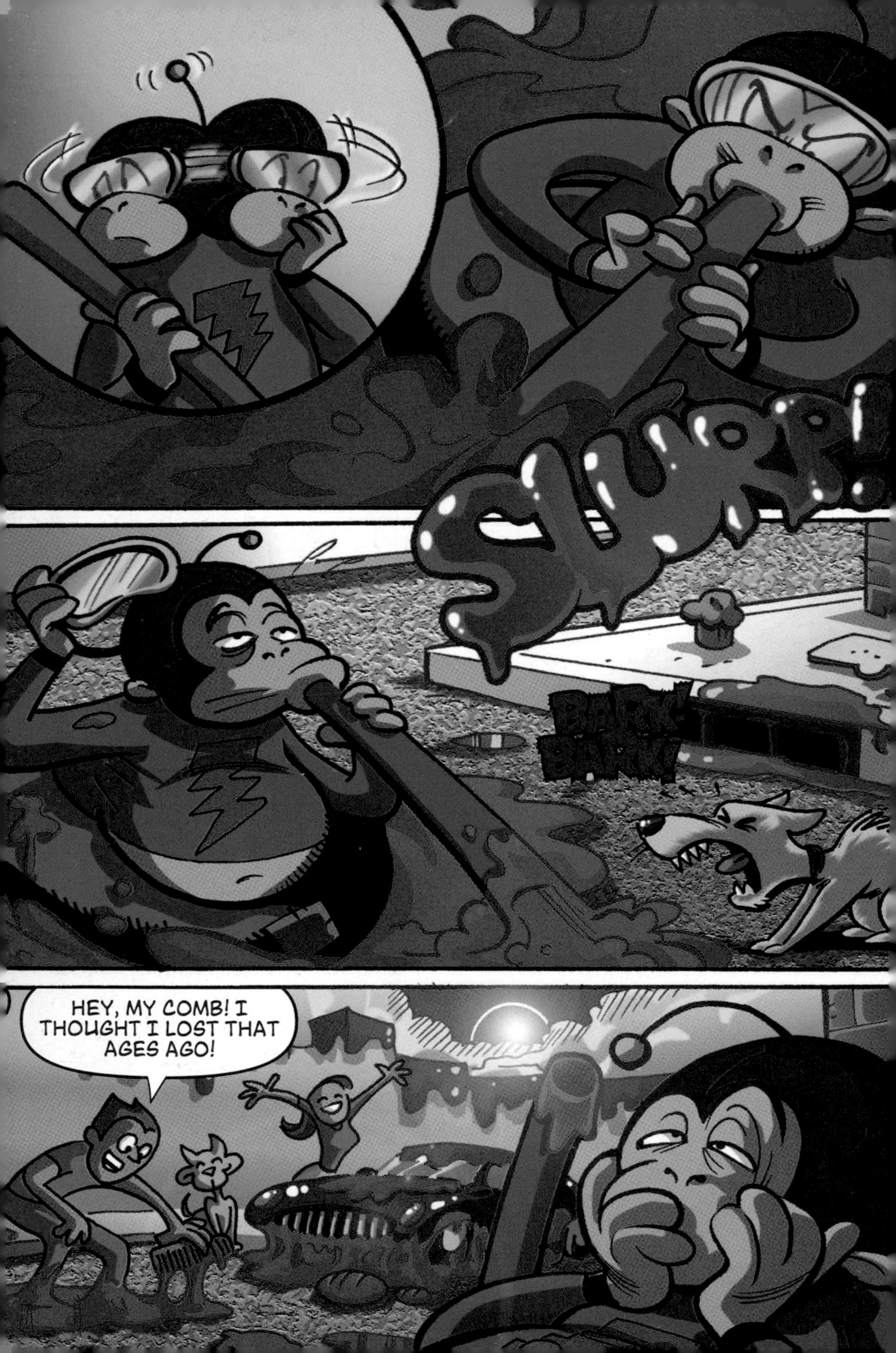
SLURP!
BARK! BARK!
HEY, MY COMB! I THOUGHT I LOST THAT AGES AGO!

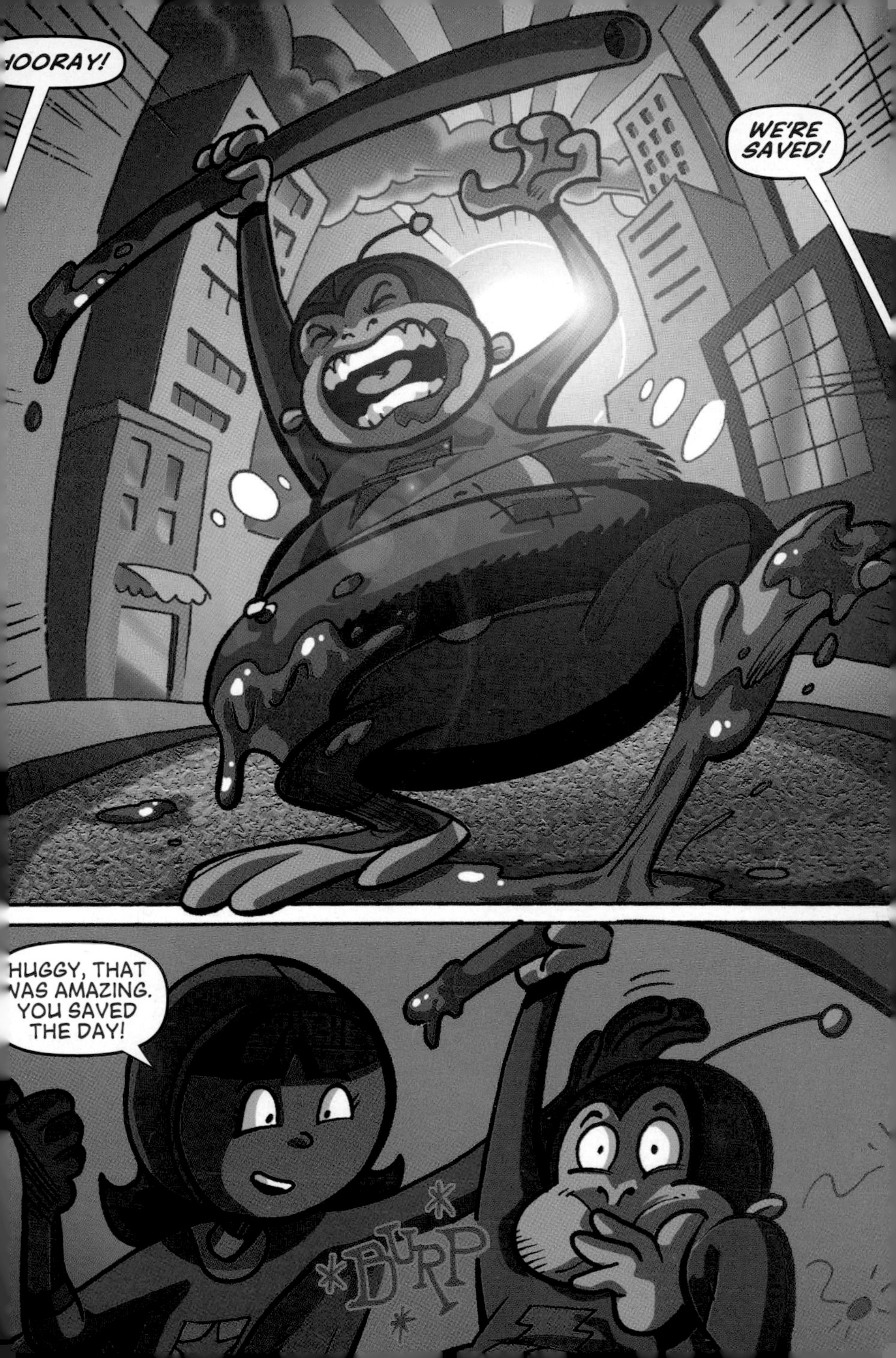
HOORAY!
WE'RE SAVED!
HUGGY, THAT WAS AMAZING. YOU SAVED THE DAY!
BURP

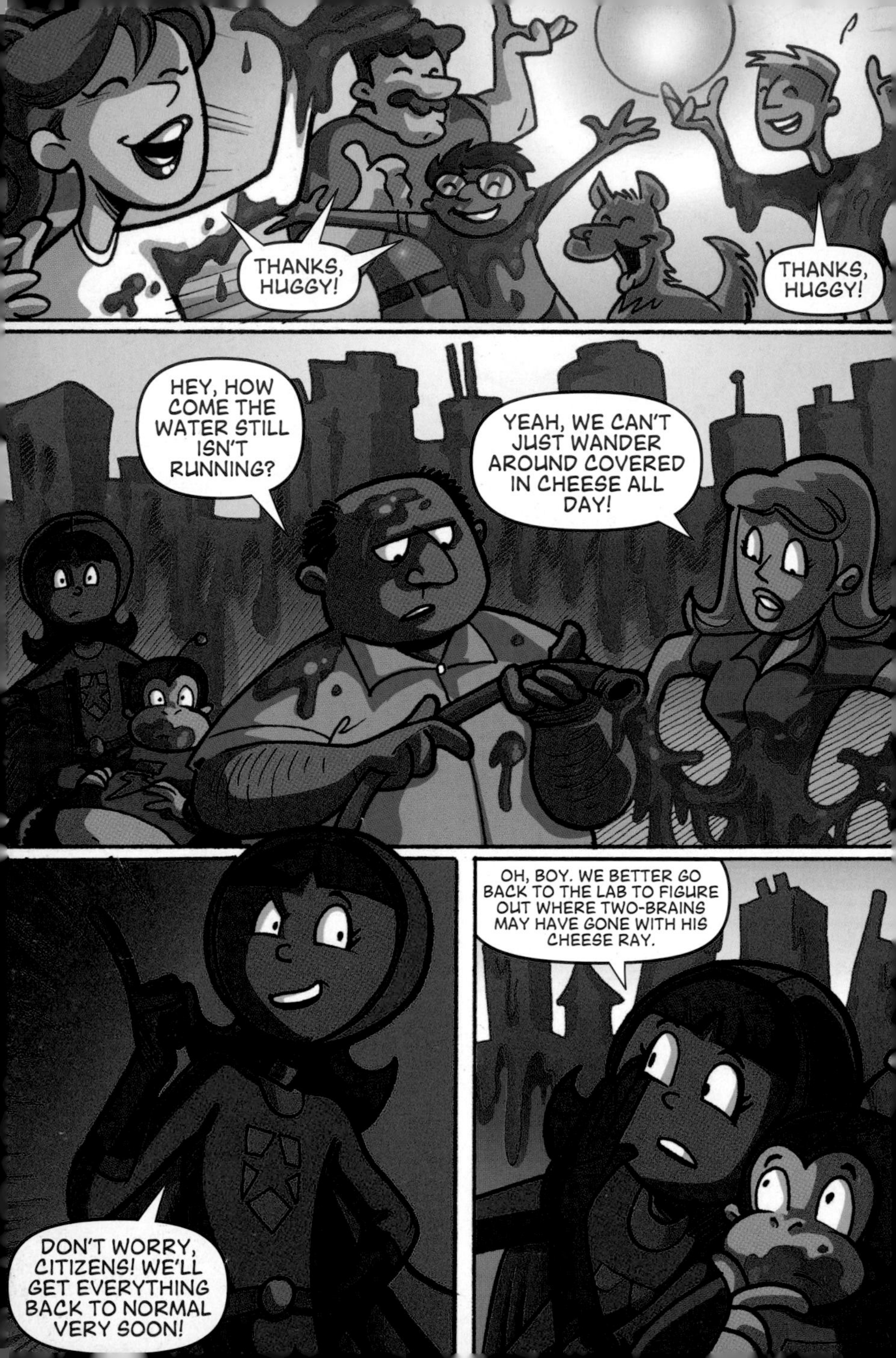
THANKS, HUGGY!
THANKS, HUGGY!
HEY, HOW COME THE WATER STILL ISN'T RUNNING?
YEAH, WE CAN'T JUST WANDER AROUND COVERED IN CHEESE ALL DAY!
DON'T WORRY, CITIZENS! WE'LL GET EVERYTHING BACK TO NORMAL VERY SOON!
OH, BOY. WE BETTER GO BACK TO THE LAB TO FIGURE OUT WHERE TWO-BRAINS MAY HAVE GONE WITH HIS CHEESE RAY.

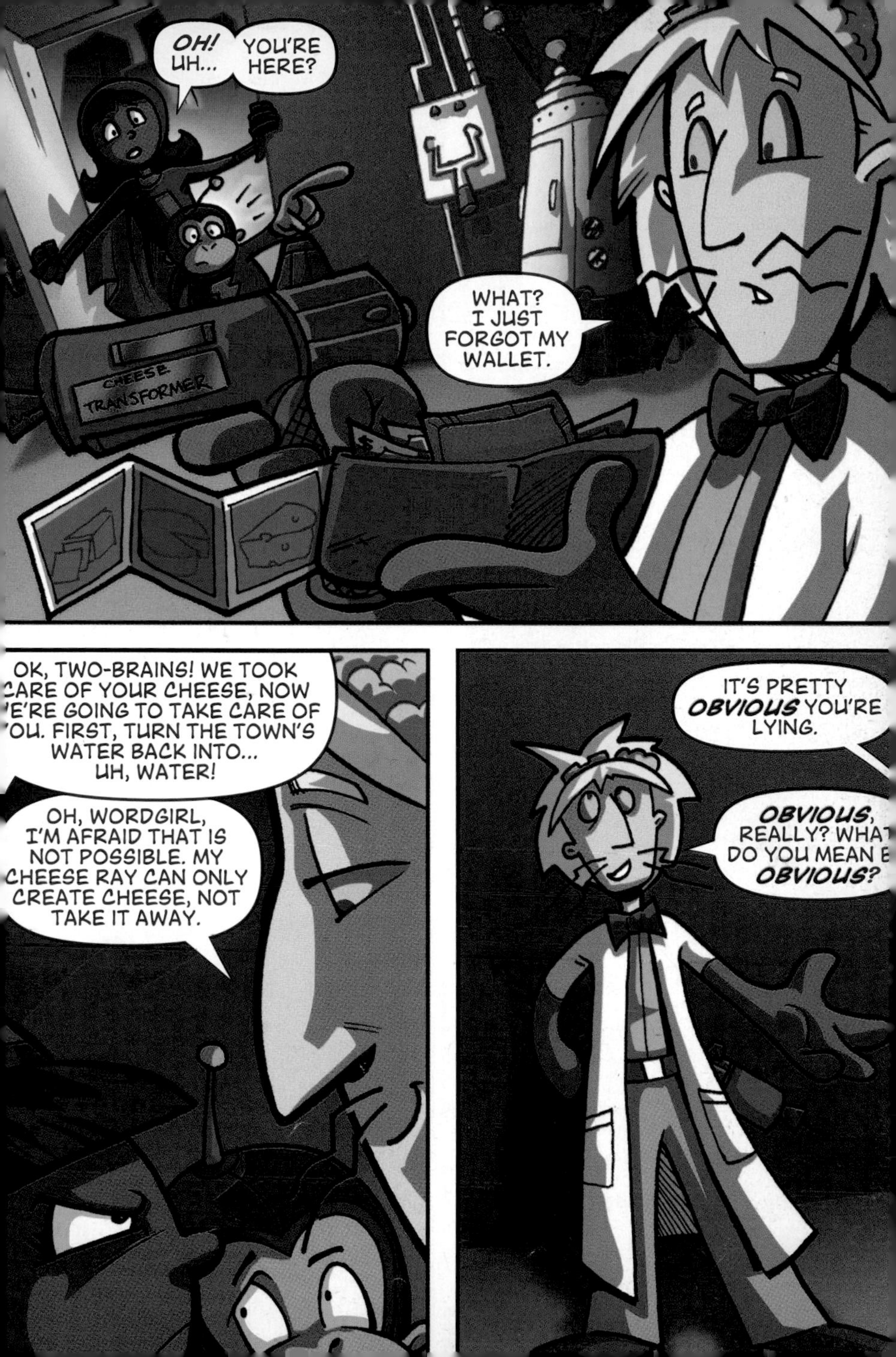
OH! UH...
YOU'RE HERE?
WHAT? I JUST FORGOT MY WALLET.
CHEESE TRANSFORMER
OK, TWO-BRAINS! WE TOOK ARE OF YOUR CHEESE, NOW 'E'RE GOING TO TAKE CARE OF 'OU. FIRST, TURN THE TOWN'S WATER BACK INTO... UH, WATER!
OH, WORDGIRL, I'M AFRAID THAT IS NOT POSSIBLE. MY CHEESE RAY CAN ONLY CREATE CHEESE, NOT TAKE IT AWAY.
IT'S PRETTY OBVIOUS YOU'RE LYING.
OBVIOUS, REALLY? WHA DO YOU MEAN B OBVIOUS?

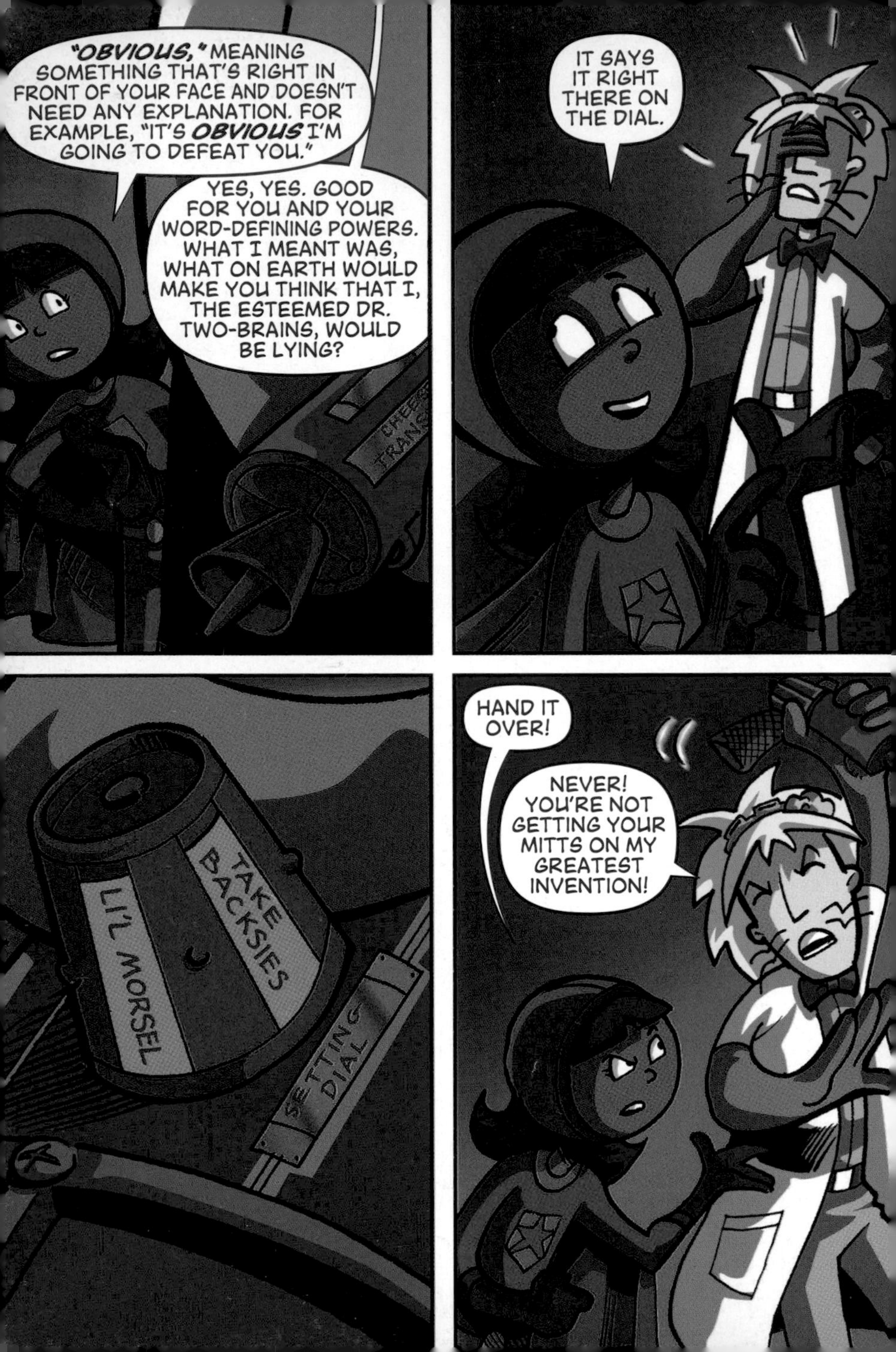
"OBVIOUS," MEANING SOMETHING THAT'S RIGHT IN FRONT OF YOUR FACE AND DOESN'T NEED ANY EXPLANATION. FOR EXAMPLE, "IT'S OBVIOUS I'M GOING TO DEFEAT YOU."
YES, YES. GOOD FOR YOU AND YOUR WORD-DEFINING POWERS. WHAT I MEANT WAS, WHAT ON EARTH WOULD MAKE YOU THINK THAT I, THE ESTEEMED DR. TWO-BRAINS, WOULD BE LYING?
IT SAYS IT RIGHT THERE ON THE DIAL.
TAKE BACKSIES
LI'L MORSEL
SETTING DIAL
HAND IT OVER!
NEVER! YOU'RE NOT GETTING YOUR MITTS ON MY GREATEST INVENTION!

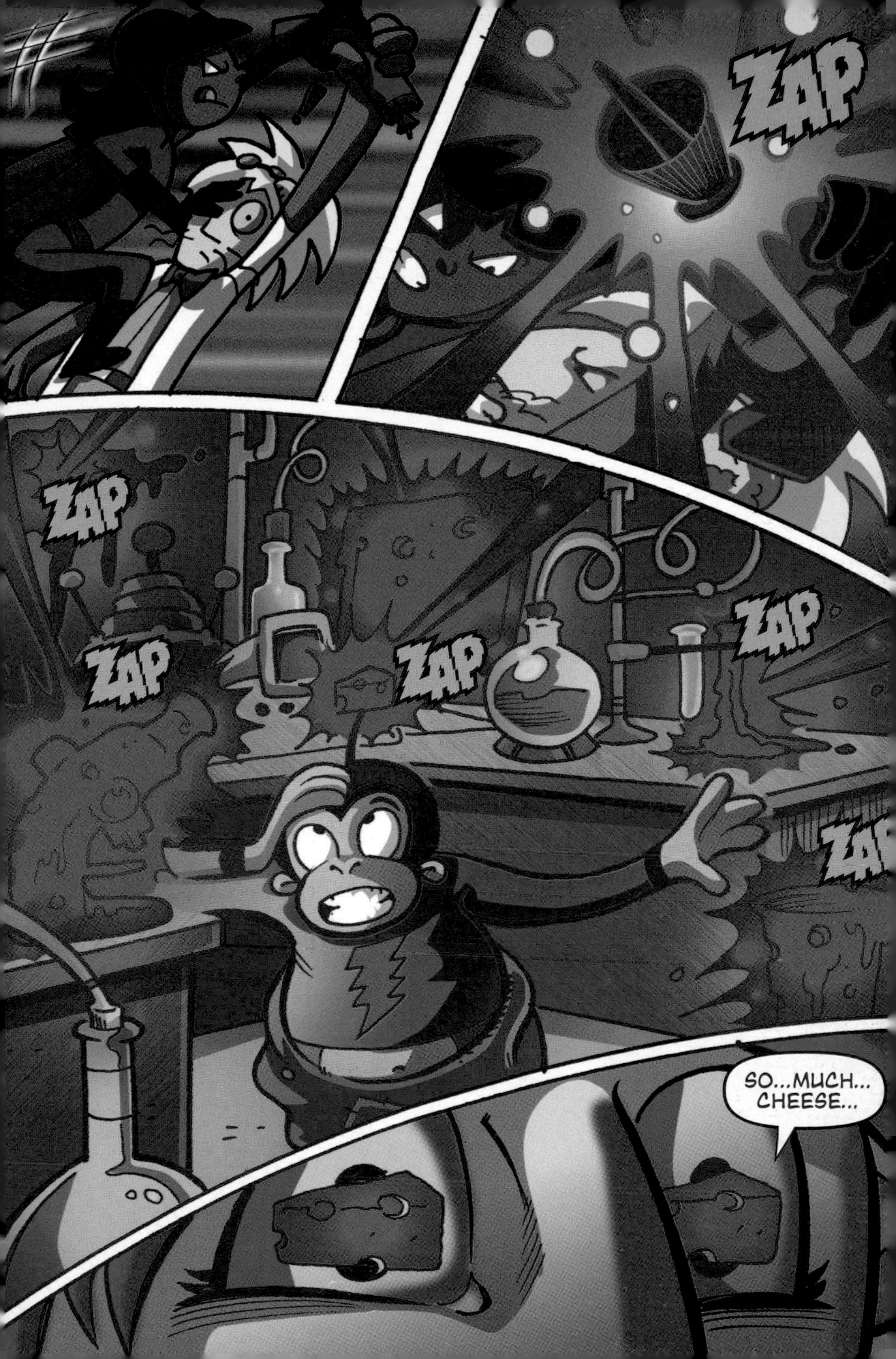
ZAP
ZAP
ZAP
ZAP
ZAP
SO...MUCH...
CHEESE...

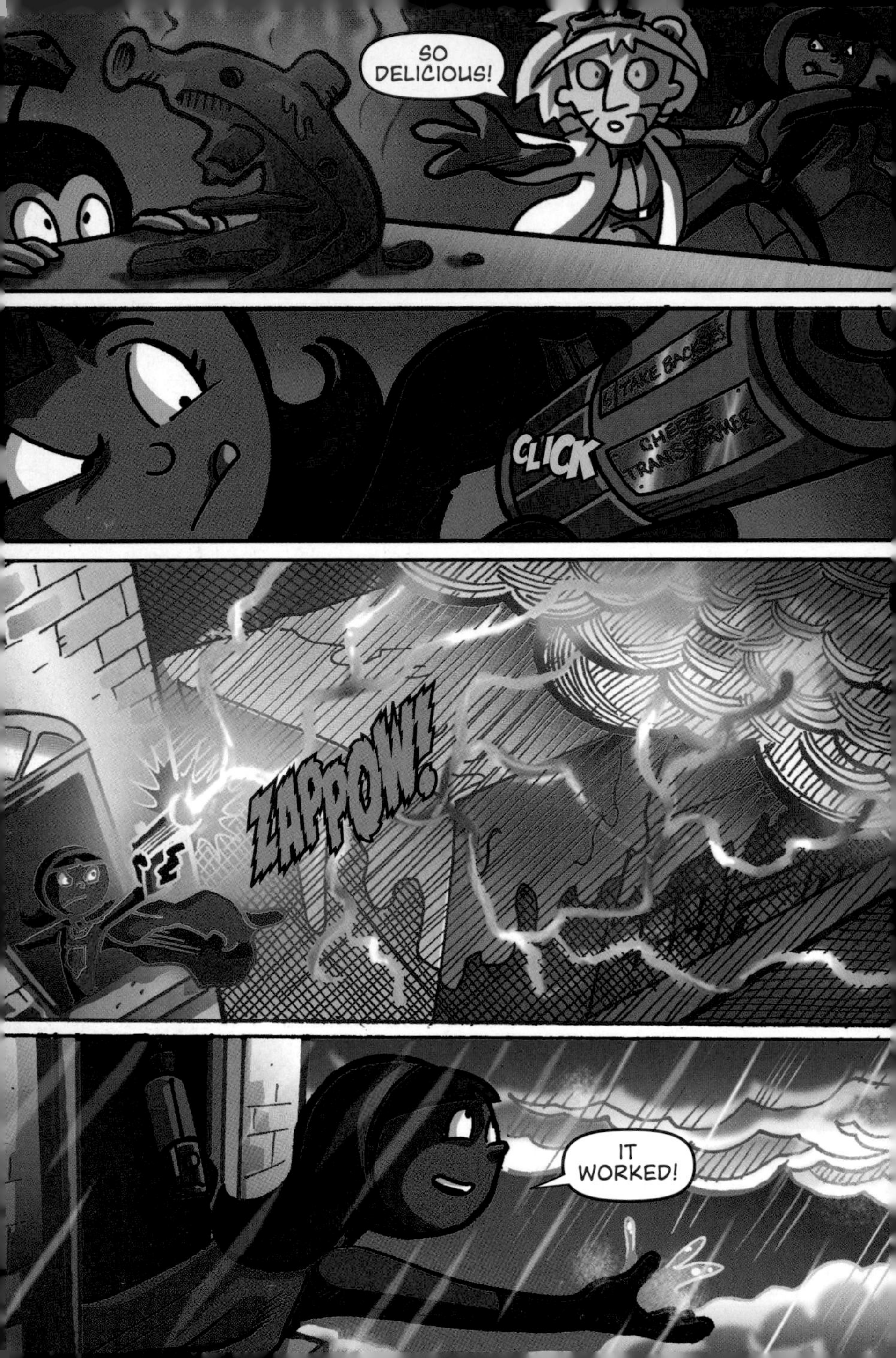
SO DELICIOUS!
CLICK
CHEESE TRANSFORMER
ZAPPOW!
IT WORKED!

RAIN?

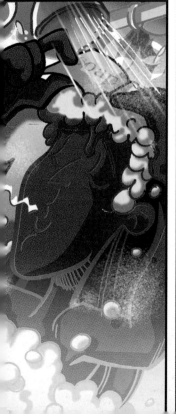

CRUMBLED JUST LIKE AN EIGHT-YEAR-OLD CHEDDAR!

CRUNCH!

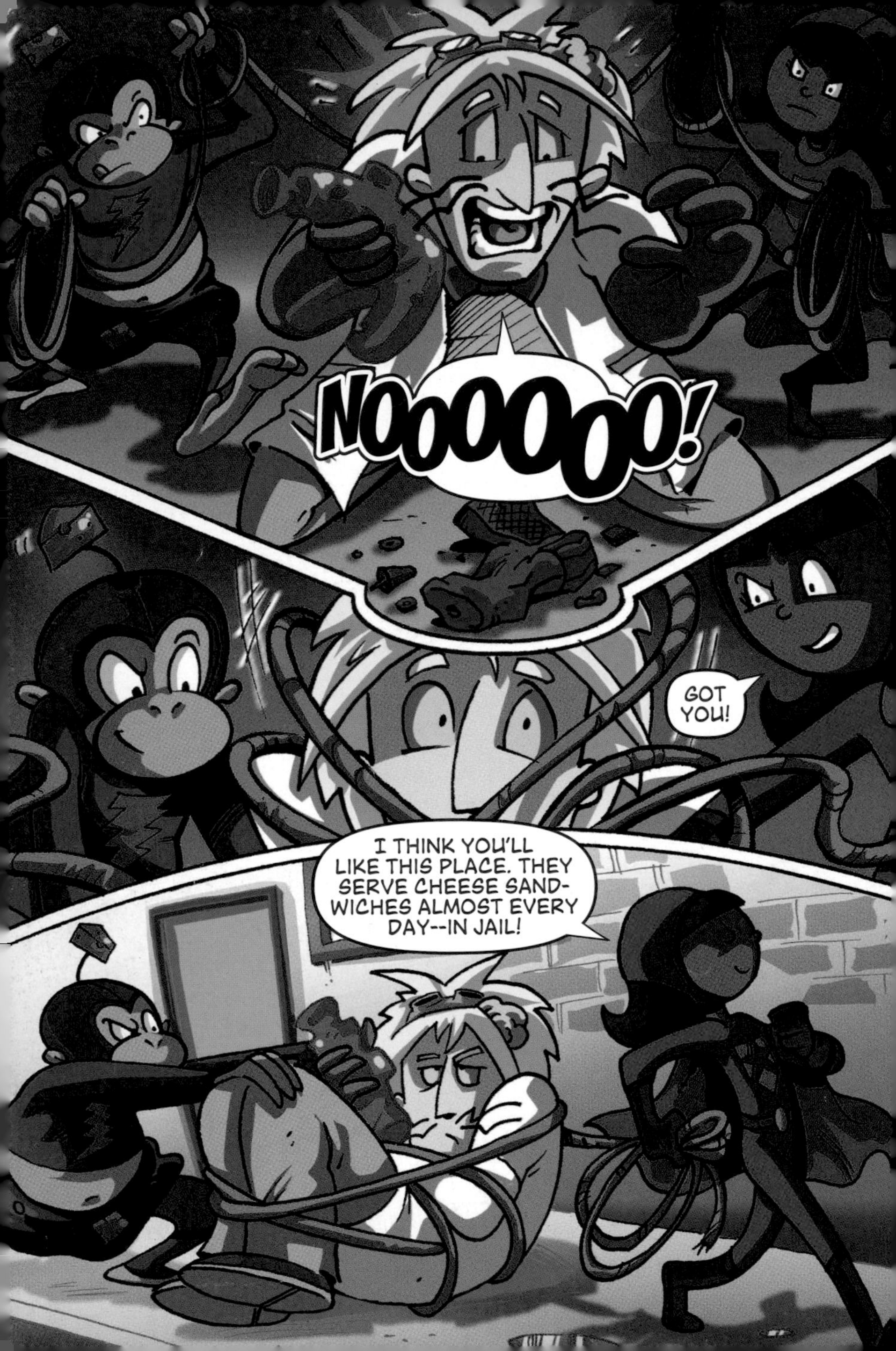
NOOOOOO!
GOT YOU!
I THINK YOU'LL LIKE THIS PLACE. THEY SERVE CHEESE SAND-WICHES ALMOST EVERY DAY--IN JAIL!

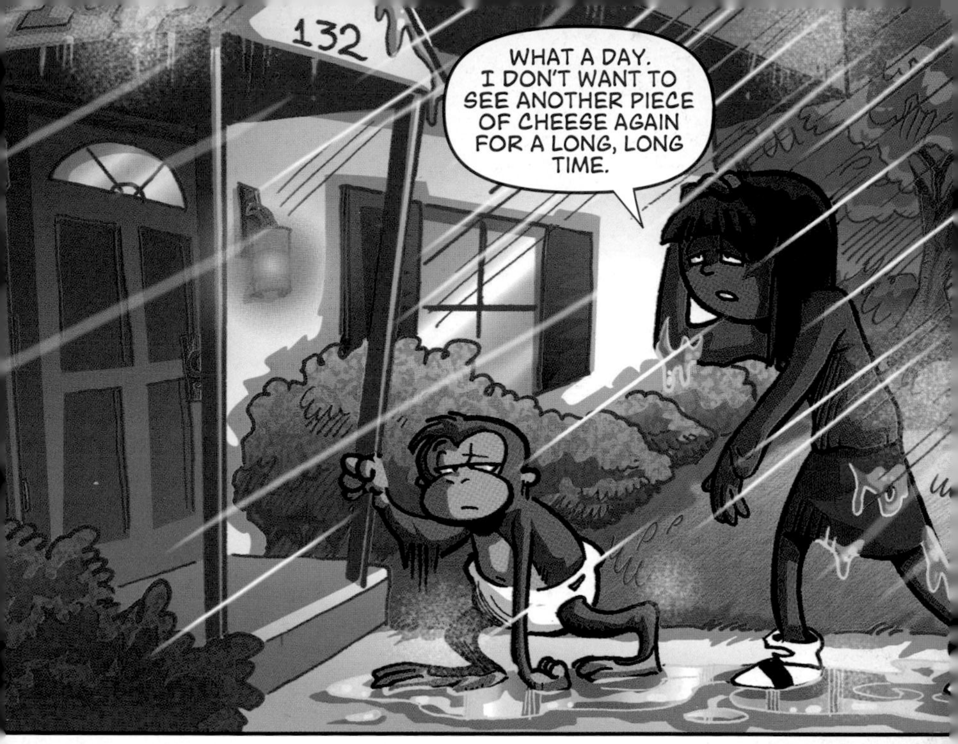
132
WHAT A DAY. I DON'T WANT TO SEE ANOTHER PIECE OF CHEESE AGAIN FOR A LONG, LONG TIME.

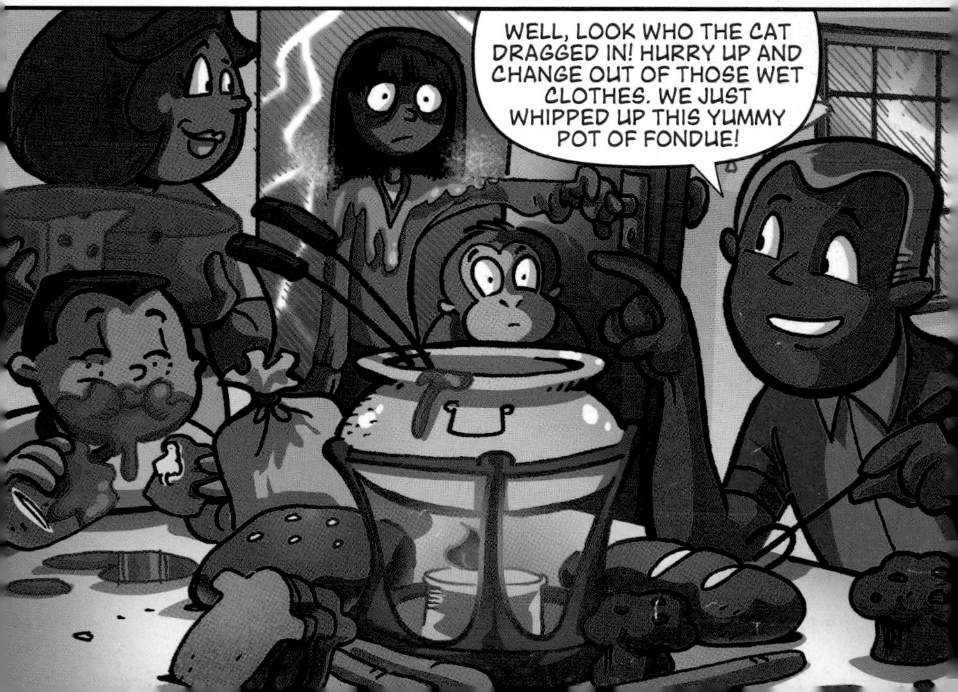
WELL, LOOK WHO THE CAT DRAGGED IN! HURRY UP AND CHANGE OUT OF THOSE WET CLOTHES. WE JUST WHIPPED UP THIS YUMMY POT OF FONDUE!

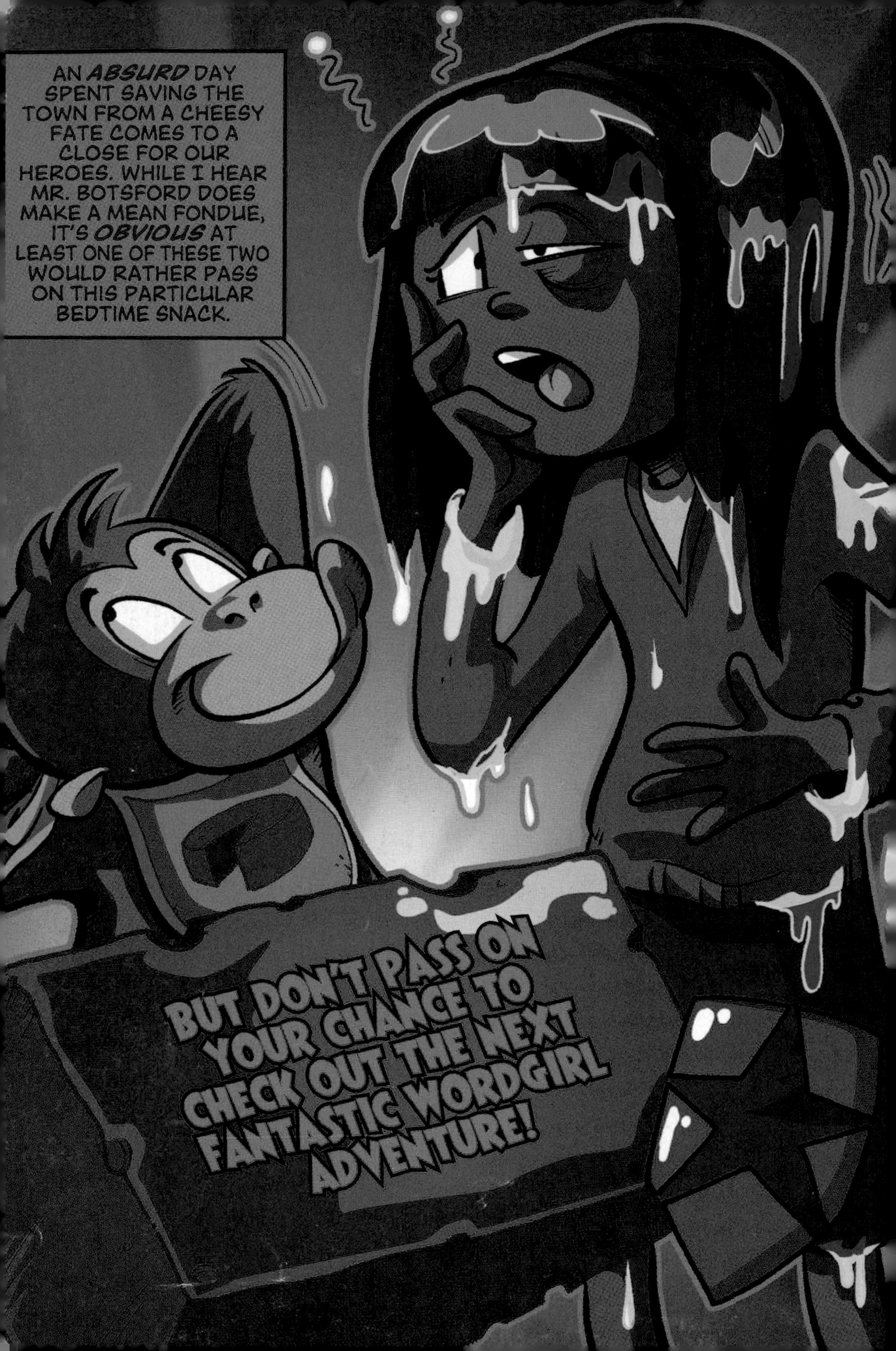
AN ABSURD DAY SPENT SAVING THE TOWN FROM A CHEESY FATE COMES TO A CLOSE FOR OUR HEROES. WHILE I HEAR MR. BOTSFORD DOES MAKE A MEAN FONDUE, IT'S OBVIOUS AT LEAST ONE OF THESE TWO WOULD RATHER PASS ON THIS PARTICULAR BEDTIME SNACK.
BUT DON'T PASS ON YOUR CHANCE TO CHECK OUT THE NEXT FANTASTIC WORDGIRL ADVENTURE!

GLOSSARY

Accustomed [uh-kuhs-tuh′md]
Frequently practiced, used, or experienced; customary.

Browse [brouz]
To look through or glance at casually.

Crumble [kruhm-buh′l]
To fall into small pieces; break or part into small fragments.

Disobedient [dis-uh-bee-dee-uh′nt]
Refusing to obey.

Encourage [en-kur-ij]
To inspire with courage, spirit, or confidence; to stimulate by approval.

Flatter [flat-er]
To try to please by complimentary remarks or attention; to praise.

Fondue [fon-doo]
A sauce-like dish of Swiss origin made with melted cheese and seasonings.

Invention [in-ven-shuh′n]
A new or improved process or machine developed through study and experimentation.

Maintain [meyn-teyn]
To keep in an appropriate condition; preserve.

Mechanical [muh-kan-i-kuh′l]
Having to do with machines or tools.

Nonsense [non-sens]
Words, conduct, or actions that are senseless, foolish, or absurd.

Obvious [ob-vee-uh's]
Easily seen, recognized, or understood.

Particular [per-tik-yuh-ler]
Of or pertaining to a single or specific person, place, or thing.

Positive [poz-i-tiv]
Emphasizing what is good or beneficial; constructive.

Predictable [prih-dik-tuh-buh'l]
Able to be foretold or declared in advance; expected.

Satisfied [sat-is-fahyd]
Filled with satisfaction or contentment.

Surrender [suh-ren-der]
To give up, abandon, or relinquish; to yield or resign to another.

Withstand [with-stand]
To hold out against; to resist or oppose successfully.